NATHALIA RUI

Falling for the Angel

A Monster Romance

To those who survived the trauma but not the aftermath,
and to those still surviving,
may your days be brighter.

Contents

Author's Note

Thank you for picking up *Falling for the Angel*!

I grew up attending an orthodox Catholic church and was always fascinated by the designs and descriptions of biblical angels (which was later amplified by my love for Bayonetta). Creating my angel was a true callback to my days sitting in the pews, imagining what angels truly looked like: multiple heads, no bodies, no limbs or extra limbs — it was a horror fan's dream!

Astamesiophelous' design is near and dear to my heart, as it's an ode to the ornate nature of the church I grew up in. I'm no longer a practicing Catholic but I'll always love stained glass, gold, and copious amounts of filigree.

As a final note: this novella is very personal to me. It's a story I've wanted to write for years, but could never find the proper words to tell it. I hope you enjoy Marcy and Asta's story.

-Nathalia Rui

Pronunciation guide:
    Astamesiophelous: AH-stuh-mes-E-O-feel-us
    Asta: AH-stuh

Helpline Info

If you or someone you know is a victim of domestic abuse, there are ways to get help.

Global:

- **RAINN: (1-800-799-7233)**

United States:

- **Crisis Text Line:** 741-741 (Text from any cell phone in the USA).
- **National Domestic Violence Hotline: (1-800-787-3224)**
- **National Sexual Assault Hotline: (1-800-656-4673)**

Content Warning

This novella contains graphic scenes, disturbing content, and dark imagery. Reader discretion is advised.

The full list is as follows:

Graphic depictions of:

- Domestic abuse
- Child abuse
- On-page death
- Blood/gore
- Religious blasphemy

Implications of (never explicitly stated, only lightly referenced or implied):

- Child loss/miscarriage
- Infertility
- Suicide and self-harm
- Sexual assault
- Forced incest

BE NOT AFRAID,
MY CHILD

Chapter 1

Marcy

Radiant light pours in from above, creating a dazzling display, the rays akin to streams of sheer fabric. They ripple in the slight breeze, contorting around one another like a couple engaged in a dance.

Marcy has never seen such breathtaking beauty.

Her mouth slides agape as she fumbles at her chest, seeking the gold cross from her necklace that lays coolly against her skin.

What is this place?

She can't seem to recall what she was doing earlier, let alone how she got here. Was she sleepwalking again? Did she take too many painkillers? Or did she get hit in the head and is concussed?

No.

Zaps prick her brain as if it were a pincushion, her memory fuzzy and missing large pieces. From what she can remember, she was at the store buying groceries, then came home to rest on the couch. Then… then…

Blank.

Panic begins to set in, the mystery of this hollow space raising the sinews at the back of her neck. She studies the room, attempting to discern her location or a recognizable exit.

The ground is stark white, as is the sky above. Her bare feet are unable to comprehend the terrain, giving the illusion that she is floating in nothingness. Her only indicator of depth is the vague shadows crawling beneath her.

"Be not afraid, my child," an echoing voice bellows, and the resonating baritones rattle deeply within Marcy's bones

"Hello? Is someone there?" she calls out, frantically searching for anything tangible in the barren room. "Where am I?"

A thin, black line forms within the fabric of white, growing larger until Marcy is eclipsed by its size. A silhouette emerges through it. It is more than twice her height, the size and shape so grandiose it could be mistaken for a building.

A cluster of vibrant feathers cut through the amorphous void, the pure white plumage dusted with cream along the pointed tips. Three pairs of wings connect to a ruffled, avian-like torso, with several crimson eyes lining the coverts of the wings. Long tail feathers drape to the floor, puddling beneath the creature as its pinions sway to keep it afloat.

Words catch in Marcy's throat, unable to fathom the striking creature that materializes before her. Terror, curiosity, and dread all barrage her nerves as she drags her gaze up to where the creature's head should be.

Should.

Its severed neck is lined with a collar of feathers, ending before any head can be formed. In the space where a face should be, a levitating ring rotates two masks, one of a bull and one of a fox. There are a handful of smaller rings that orbit the masks in a rhythmic pace.

It's paralyzing to look at. The sight of the imposing monster unsettles Marcy's stomach, causing bile to rise and burn the back of her throat.

Two human-like arms extend from the lower half of the creature's body, their skin resembling that of a starry night sky. They offer both their massive palms, careful not to get too close.

"Please, little lamb, do not worry," they say. Their disembodied voices are gentle and give the assurance of peace. "You are safe. You will not be hurt."

Marcy does not take their offered hands.

She twists her fingers in the chain of her necklace, then pulls it tighter as a bead of sweat builds on her temple.

She repeats her earlier question, nausea drawing saliva to the corners of her mouth, "Where am I?"

The being does not lower their spread palms, despite her rejection. Each individual eye on the wings focus on Marcy with intent, eyelashes fluttering with every blink.

"You are in the afterlife."

A gargled, choked gasp falls from Marcy's lips, her eyebrows rising to kiss her hairline. Her knees weaken, and the tremble in her hands increase, becoming tremors as she sinks to the ground.

"I'm… *dead?*" she whispers in disbelief. She cannot be *dead*; she's only thirty-six years old, much too young to succumb to death.

The creature approaches cautiously, the ring above their neck tilting inquisitively. "Correct. Your physical body has perished, and your soul has arrived in the afterlife."

A look of horror crosses her expression, frown lines deepening. Her eyes dart in every direction, and she blinks rapidly, as if willing it to all disappear.

"Ah!" they start, a new realization in their voice. Although their tone changes, the faces of the masks remain static. "I apologize. There has been a misunderstanding. *This* is not the afterlife." Their hands shape a circle, gesturing broadly in emphasis.

She sighs in momentary relief, but it's soon ripped away as the creature resumes speaking.

"You will not be spending eternity *here*." They motion with their hands again. "This is only the evaluation chamber. So please, do not fret."

They speak as if this clarification somehow improves Marcy's circumstances.

I'm not dead. I must be on the couch, dreaming.

"You are not dreaming."

No.

"No?" they ask, repeating her thoughts aloud.

Stop.

"Stop what?" They stare at her with childlike curiosity, seemingly unable to understand why she is panicking.

Pain radiates in waves throughout her skull when the creature invades her thoughts. It feels like a torrid grip seizing her brain.

"Stop reading my mind!" she shouts in frustration, clawing at her scalp.

Marcy's quivering hands move to cover her face, grief spilling over as tears flow from her eyes in an uncontrollable torrent.

"Oh, I, um," the creature worries, their voice shrinking to a whisper. "I did not mean to upset you. I will stop reading your mind if that is what—"

"If this is not a dream, then return me to my body," she demands, hiccupping and gasping through her tears.

I can't be dead. I need to go home.

There's a mess to clean, dinner to cook, and laundry to fold. He'll forgive me, just like he always does, if I make his favorite meal and—

A chilled hand strokes Marcy's shoulder. She recoils, her gaze snapping to the display of masks and eyes examining her with pity.

"You can never go back. Your body is gone."

Marcy has no reason to distrust the being's words, but she can't seem to comprehend the truth, even if the creature's existence and resplendent appearance are sufficient proof. If she does happen to be passed out, hallucinating, or having a nightmare, she should be able to wake herself up.

Taking the tender skin at the back of her hand between her nails, she pinches it hard. She sucks her teeth from the pain but digs in until a bead of blood appears.

A familiar cool touch dares to brush against her once more, a disembodied hand materializing from a ring that strayed from the creature's body.

"Why are you hurting yourself?" they question, concerned.

She pushes away from the creature's touch with a subtle flinch.

This isn't a dream, she thinks, although the realization doesn't truly sink in. If it did, she might vomit.

Backing away a minuscule yet comfortable distance, she demands in a wavering voice, "Tell me who you are."

The creature looks pleased, clasping their hands together. Their feathered chest lifts in a sigh of relief at her momentary compliance. "I am called Astamesiophelous. Humankind would refer to me as an 'angel.'"

"You look nothing like an angel," she replies quickly, tone laced with skepticism. "You're..."

"A monster?" they supply, amused. "Humans tend to take comfort in portraying ethereal beings like themselves by mirroring their own habits, features, and flaws. But none of that is true." They press their index finger to their chest, drawing their wings inward. "I could not find a form you found appealing while searching your memories, but I can change my shape if that would please you."

Shaking her head, her tawny colored locks spill from the pins that keep them fastened tightly against her scalp.

"No, it's alright. I find your current appearance to be somewhat pleasant," she says, leaving out *'at a distance.'* Even though the creature is an imposing force, she doesn't deny the beauty in both their appearance and gentle disposition.

They pause, wings stilling in the air. "You don't want me to look like anyone else? Are you certain?"

She's more than certain — there isn't a single person she wishes to see, and it would be a waste of time trying to think of one.

"Yes, I am sure, Astema— Astumes—"

"You may refer to me as Asta, little lamb," they say with a silky chuckle. Heat rises in Marcy's cheeks.

"Thank you, Asta," she says, tucking a stray hair behind her ear. "But, uh… are you a man, or a woman? How should I refer to you?"

Though they have no true face, Marcy notes the dumbfounded expression their essence portrays when they explain, "I have no sex. I am neither a man nor a woman, yet I am everything in between."

Marcy contorts her face in a nervous grimace. "Meaning…?"

"Choose whichever pronoun you prefer. He, they, she, it — it is up to you," Asta concedes and attempts to offer their enormous hand again.

Marcy eyes the expanse of their palm, turning the idea of placing her hand atop theirs around in her head.

"May I refer to you as a male? In prayer, I'm quite used to that," she mumbles.

"Of course, if that pleases you."

A silent moment passes between them, the heaviness of her uncertainty palpable. Despite her prying, keen stare, Asta waits patiently for her decision.

Not much more can go wrong at this point. I'm already dead. I don't really have a choice but to trust him.

Pressing her lips together in a frown, she decides to accept his touch. Gingerly, she slips her hand into his, bracing herself for the expected unpleasant feel of his skin.

When their palms collide, a sudden shiver runs down her spine. The electricity between them draws a deep sigh from the depths of her chest. Her skin brushes against Asta's, his opposing texture almost ticklish.

"If this is part of the afterlife, am I in Heaven?" she asks.

Swallowing her tiny hand within his own, Asta assists Marcy from her meek position on the floor. "There is no such thing as Heaven," he replies.

A grave look draws her brows together, forming a crease along her forehead. "I'm going to Hell? But I prayed. I was a faithful, loving wife, I did everything—"

"There is no Hell, either."

She cocks her head.

Asta chuckles again, the sound filled with more delight than before. He lays another hand on top of hers, and the tingling sensation increases, racing up and down the length of her arms.

"You humans are very creative, but there is no such thing as eternal punishment. Your soul may be reconstructed, but it's certainly not through torture." For a moment, his eyes flash with red light, appearing entertained. "The gods are not cruel."

"*Gods*? Plural?" Marcy nearly shouts. The revelation is almost as astonishing as learning she's dead. Can there truly be more than one God...?

"There is no way for me to explain it in a way you could comprehend. Any further clarification, and your very being may unravel," he explains, effortlessly lifting Marcy into his arms. "I will continue to answer your questions, but we need to begin reviewing your memories. Humans can't exist in the ethereal realm for extended periods of time, and I want to be sure that I allow you a proper evaluation."

She nods, but her mind is reeling from an onslaught of inquiries that never seem to make it past her lips. As they float through the swirling ribbons of light, a single sentence repeats through her thoughts, growing louder until it becomes impossible to ignore.

"Who are you?"

His arms twitch beneath her, evidently surprised at the abruptness of her question. "I thought I already answered that."

"Ah, no," she shakes her head. "I meant, what do you do? In church, they'd teach us about the many roles of different angels. Angels have tasks, don't they?"

Asta hums. "Some do; some don't."

"Let me guess, the real answer is something I can't comprehend?" she says with a small laugh. The levity with which she speaks surprises her. Her previous discomfort starts to dissipate in the peculiar reassurance of Asta's arms.

A ghost of a smile dances in his voice when he replies, "No, but the classifications are exceptionally boring. Or so I have been told by the previous humans who have asked."

"Well, I'm asking. About you, specifically," she says, scanning the strange black rings that encircle a larger one near his neck.

Any lightness in his previous tone is replaced by solemnity. He speaks with authority, as if presenting himself before a crowd.

"I am what is known as the Evaluator. My purpose is to objectively evaluate your life and determine where your soul belongs in the afterlife. I will judge if your soul needs to be reconstructed, or if you are free to become one with the universe again."

Unaware of her wandering hands, Marcy runs her fingers lazily across Asta's chest. The stubby feathers carry the same downy, tender softness as the surface of water. The sensation is unique, causing her heart to flutter.

"Are you listening, little lamb?"

Startled, she gazes up at his masks, unsure of where to focus. Heat rises along her cheeks at being caught staring.

"Ah, yes, you are… an evaluator?"

"Correct. During my evaluation, we will review your life together through a finite number of memories. Afterward, once all is witnessed, I will do as my title describes," he says.

Review my life?

The taste of copper spreads over her tongue. She tries to swallow down the horrid flavor, but she can't seem to lessen it.

Review.

Relive.

Review my life.

Asta snaps his fingers, and a dark line forms from above, bowing out into a circular void. It's just as large as the one he initially appeared from. The pitch darkness inside is eerie against the pure white environment.

He carries Marcy through the strange-looking shadow, seemingly unbothered by the disorientation it causes.

As light begins to fill the space around them, a familiar unease twists her gut. Blurry visions of a beach start to arrange themselves from geometric shapes, but the colors are both muted and bizarre.

A structure sits along the grass line. The dilapidated building is covered with a coat of hastily applied paint on the chipped siding, which does little to protect it from the elements. Connected to the porch is a splintered wooden swing, its metal hooks shrieking with rust.

Threads of shame pull tight, and Marcy buries her face within the ruffled feathers of Asta's breast.

"I don't want to review my life," she murmurs, the beating in her chest growing louder. "Send me to wherever you see fit. I'll accept it without complaint, I promise."

Marcy's feet touch sand as Asta lowers her, the hollow sounds of a roaring ocean overwhelming the calm scene. No birds are chirping, no animals scurry about. There is nothing to indicate any signs of life other than her own.

"This is not a choice," he reminds her with a soft-hearted drawl.

She claps her hands over her ears, squeezing her eyes shut. With her head shaking vehemently, a wave of nausea draws sweat along her chin.

"No!" she shouts through the knot lodged in her throat. "I don't want to remember. Please, God, don't make me...."

The crashing ocean waves halt, and Marcy's hands are forced from her ears as though compelled. It's not painful, but they are pulled down to her thighs with a loud *slap*.

Asta towers over her, his many eyes softening around the edges. "I apologize for influencing your mind, Marcy, but I need you to listen to me. You are not alone. I will bear witness to your most vulnerable moments alongside you. This is the way of evaluation. There is no avoiding it."

"But why? What's the point? Make your judgment now. Just get it over with," she pleads, hugging her arms to her chest after Asta relinquishes control. "Living through it all once was enough."

Sighing, Asta cradles her face in his hand, turning her chin toward him. Although his thumb is large enough to cover the entirety of her jaw, he soothes her trembling with a delicate swipe across her cheek, whisking away her newly formed tears.

"For me to understand the versions of you that exist in both your best and worst moments, I must *feel* them through you." His words are soft, dancing lightly to avoid sounding stern. "I will not criticize you. Part of my goal is to bring you peace."

Marcy opens her mouth to protest, but Asta is quicker.

"Will you allow me your trust, little lamb?"

Her cheeks puff with a pout, and she blinks away the moisture welling in her eyes. Trust is something she's never given to anyone, since it always ends up broken in the end. Asta is patient with her though, and given his position of power, he doesn't need to be. It brings her a shred of solace, but it hardly lessens the sting of being forced to face all of the abject horrors she was a victim to throughout her mortal life.

But like he so kindly reminded her, she does not have a choice.

Her thoughts race as the sound of Asta's beating wings fills her ears, and she presses her palm against his fingers. The chilled galaxies of his flesh burst with light when the corners of her lips curl upward.

All she needs to do is get through the memory. Get through it. Get to the end.

The end.

She swallows hard, her jaw ticking in preparation.

"Okay, Asta," Marcy sighs. "Let's go see Father."

Chapter 2

Astamesiophelous

"This is only a memory. You will not be able to interact with anyone," Asta explains, watching Marcy hesitate to open the door.

Her brows pinch in worry as she glances at him over her shoulder. Words hang on her tongue, and after a few seconds, she whispers, "I'm sorry if this is disturbing for you to watch."

The rings of Asta's head wobble, indicating his version of a smile. "You needn't worry about me, little lamb. 'Angels' don't have emotions."

'Shouldn't' is the correct word, he thinks, a pang of anxiety needling his chest.

Marcy's nod is reserved, but her soft lips lift into a small smile as the lines of her forehead smooth. She twists the handle to open the door, then steps inside the sparsely decorated cabin.

The scents of cigarette smoke and whiskey linger in the air, suffocating the light aroma from the wilted flowers sitting on the dining table.

Asta hums, assessing the empty bottles and dirty clothing littered atop the carpet. "Is this your childhood home?" he asks.

Blurry photos hang in crooked frames on the walls, Marcy's memory too weak to recall the images in them. Family photos, possibly.

"No," she says, her eyes glazing over with indifference. "This is where Father took my brother and me when Mother went on her retreats."

"Retreats?"

Marcy nods slowly, her lips pursed. "She often went away with her Bible study group. It was supposed to 'reinvigorate' her when Father thought she was not performing to his standards." She does not attempt to hide the bitterness in her tone.

"I see," Asta comments, unwilling to press further at the risk of troubling her. "Shall we start?"

Marcy consents in the form of a single-note hum, carefully steeling herself.

Asta snaps his fingers.

Before them appear two figures: a young girl, no more than the age of ten, and an older man with a patch of hair missing from the crown of his skull. The man drinks a deep brown liquid from a crystal glass. A lit cigarette hangs from his mouth while music plays from a record player in the corner.

"Marce! Where's dinner?" he shouts, eyes glued to the black and white television screen.

The young girl audibly struggles to lift a pan from inside the oven, but the older man does not move to help. He instead takes a swig of his drink before calling for her again.

"It'll be ready soon, Father!" she replies, out of breath from the exertion. "It needs to cool off for a moment." Silverware clatters on the table as she huffs, frantic, aware of her father's stoked irritation.

The man snorts, lolling his head back against the recliner. "You can thank your mother for not preparing food before her little 'vacation,'" he grumbles. "But that's why she needs the damn thing in the first place."

"Yes, Father," the girl says, dangling a fork over the third placemat. "Will Mitchell be joining us?"

"Nope. He's at the shooting range with your cousins."

A look of absolute dread weighs heavily on the girl's face. Cheeks that should be rosy and plump are instead gaunt and pale, and her sparse hair is tightly tied in a braided updo.

As the little girl turns to move the pan from the top of the stove to the table, Asta senses Marcy go tense beside him. When he looks at her, she is visibly bracing herself, her expression stoic.

Asta looks back at the little girl before there is a sudden *crash*, then a *clatter*.

The food she was carrying from the oven is now sprawled across the floor with the pan lying overturned beside it. Roast carrots roll into the living room, catching the older man's attention. His stony gaze slides from the television to the orange vegetables.

Frozen, the little girl's breath hitches. "Father, the pan was still hot — I'm sorry, it was an accident."

The older man jumps from his chair, dropping the crystal glass to the carpet and spilling its contents.

"What the fuck, Marce?" His rage is unlike anything Asta has seen before, especially over something so minor. "I swear you're as useless as your goddamn mother. Can't do anything right!" he shouts, thundering toward the child with his hand raised. His cumbrous steps rattle the silverware against the worn wooden table, a low growl emitting from his throat.

"I'm sorry! It was an accident! Please, I didn't mean it!"

"Now what the fuck am I supposed to eat?" He raises his arm higher as the little girl cowers in fear. "Hell, I bet you did this on purpose, didn't you? Just to piss me off."

"No!" she cries, tears streaming down her cheeks. Sniffles muddle her sentence as she says again, "I'm sorry."

"Stop cowering and stand up straight. Don't hide your face."

Through meager hesitation, the girl does as she's told, gripping her food-covered dress between her fists.

The older man's hand comes down fast, stiff as a board.

Before Asta realizes it, his hand juts out from where it rests to shield Marcy's eyes the moment the older man's hand collides with the little girl's cheek. The reflexive action draws a gasp, his eyes widening.

A deluge of protectiveness rushes through him. He's horrified at what he's witnessing. His wings quiver with anger. Channeling Marcy's soul, he realizes that his distress is not a reflection of her own. He senses nothing from her. No wallowing or self-pity, no anger, nor anything to indicate that she is upset. Only a void of loneliness.

His chest hollows, a profound emptiness draining the swirling melancholy that could split his heart in two.

It's.... painful. These feelings are painful.

Marcy stares at him with a nonchalant expression as the repeated sounds of slaps echo against the walls. "Aren't I supposed to bear witness? Why are you covering my eyes?" she asks sheepishly, though looking relieved at not needing to watch.

Yes, you are. How foolish of me.

Tsk.

Lowering his hand for Marcy to catch the final slap, he does not provide an answer. That would only complicate things.

The memory suddenly shifts, morphing away from the kitchen until it resembles a dreary bedroom. It's the same day, but it's now later in the evening.

The little girl kneels beside a bed with a rosary clutched between her tiny hands. A beam of moonlight illuminates dainty features that are now obscured by swelling and an assortment of awful colors. Blood dots both the front and back of her dress.

Mumbling a prayer, she releases a sob every few words. She shifts uncomfortably, tugging at the fabric that clings to her abdomen.

"Give me the strength to be a better daughter. I make a lot of mistakes, and while Father does his best to correct me, I still upset him." She hiccups, her voice lowering to nothing more than a breath. "All I want is for my mother to smile when she returns home. I miss her flamboyant dresses, the way she used to twirl with me before breakfast, and her singing voice. Please, God, I pray that you forgive my sins and help me become less burdensome to my parents so that they may find happiness again."

The little girl continues her prayer, but Marcy is no longer beside Asta. He startles at the realization, rushing from the bedroom. Emerging before her, he holds out a hand to halt her steps. "Where are you going?"

Marcy's gaze focuses on the floor. She shrugs, displaying the same indifference as before. "I prayed all night. That's the rest of the memory. Do we really need to stay and watch it all?"

Yes, we do.

She tilts her head, slowly dragging her gaze up his body until it lands on the ring with his masks. Her captivating golden-brown eyes are pleading, the sullen shadows beneath her lashes dark from sleepless nights filled with memories she wishes were long forgotten.

Within those pools of rich mahogany lies a coldness unlike the affection he senses in her soul. The emptiness is unsettling, yet more than recognizable. Almost like a mirror.

She's like me.

He shakes himself, ashamed of his thoughts.

"If you believe we have seen all that we need to, we can move on to the next memory," he says as a familiar squeeze tightens his chest.

A slight, timid smile forms, her earlier discomfort disappearing. "Before we go, may I see the beach one last time?" she asks shyly.

Again with those pleading eyes of hers.

Asta knows he should say no, but he doesn't. He's too intrigued by her behavior, curious to a fault.

"Yes, you may."

He snaps, and their surroundings begin to shift, the current memory shredding apart like ripping fabric. The quiet beach emerges, as does the salty, fishy smell of the ocean, causing Marcy to scrunch her button nose.

Sand gives way under her feet as the image solidifies, eliciting a giggle of delight that drifts away on a gentle gust of wind. She excitedly plops down to sit, staring out at the bright blue waves with a contented grin.

She stares up at Asta expectantly, patting the sand beside her. "Please, sit with me. If that's even possible," she says, inhaling the sea air. The tension in her body diminishes each time she fills her lungs. The scene appears nostalgic to her.

Drifting such that the rings of his head are closer, Asta accepts her request for companionship. He doesn't see a point in watching the ocean waves, since it's not real, but a twinge within his mind tells him not to point it out.

Marcy relaxes, her shoulders slouching as her pinched features soften. She may not be at peace with her death, but her expression carries less sorrow. For now.

Drawing her legs to her chest, Marcy rests her chin on her knees. She peers at Asta from the corner of her eye, tracing the lines of his feathers with her gaze.

"So, what does it mean to reincarnate a soul? If that's what ends up happening to me, I mean," she asks.

"Are you certain you want to know the answer?" His question comes out heavier than intended. He fears her demeanor may sour upon learning the truth, and he much prefers her smile and the kindness in her eyes, both of which make him feel at ease.

She shrugs a shoulder. "My soul is either reconstructed or reincarnated, correct?"

Spinning his wrist in a circle, Asta wonders how to explain the concept. It's a shame that many words of the ethereal tongue cannot be accurately translated into any human language.

"Reincarnation is the closest description, but the process is not so simple. In short, your soul will return to the mortal realm, and the energy it carries will collect into a new form of life. That new life could be any living being throughout your universe," Asta explains, gesturing to illustrate the flowing motion of her soul's energy.

"Hm," she grunts before hollowing her cheeks.

To his satisfaction, she accepts this explanation, and the chilling weight he sits with lifts ever so slightly.

Waves encroach on the patch of sand where they sit, but Marcy does not seem to mind the frigid water skimming her toes.

"And what about reconstruction?"

Asta was hoping she'd forget that part.

"It's similar to reincarnation, but your energy is used... differently," he says, keeping his voice mild.

As he feared, Marcy continues to prod.

"How so? I understand if it's something I can't comprehend, but I'd appreciate it if you'd try to explain," she says, twirling a stray piece of her hair between her fingers.

Asta does not like the anxious expression she makes but forces himself to reply anyway.

"If you are reconstructed, it means your energy, your very soul, is dismantled to its core. Any trace of who you are or used to be is wiped from existence. You are then dispersed to rejoin the world, anew. Your energy will be used to form new souls, ones yet untouched by the cycle of reincarnation." Speaking these words to Marcy, knowing it may be her fate, is disheartening.

"So, I'd become one with the universe again. That's comforting."

If Asta didn't know any better, he'd think she was trying to keep herself from... smiling? Nothing he said should evoke mirth or happiness, but the corners of her lips twitch anyway.

Perking up, she begins to trace an asymmetrical circle in the sand with her index finger. "Do you make the final decision?"

He does not intend to sound satirical, but his comment comes out that way, nonetheless. "Yes, I am the Evaluator."

She snickers, then quickly covers her mouth to appear serious. "Once you're finished with my evaluation, what will you do after this, Asta? Evaluate other souls forever? Or do you get a break?"

The question comes out of nowhere, catching Asta by surprise. He didn't think she'd be curious about him or his role. Most humans are too preoccupied with their own fate to ask. Then again, humans always find a way to surprise him. That's what he loves about them the most.

Tapping his fingertips together in a slow rhythm, he contemplates the best way to respond. He needn't lie, but something about telling her the truth twists his gut.

He's evaluated thousands — no, *millions* — of souls without issue, but Marcy's is peculiar, making him feel odd. Her soul is as bright as a star, yet she wears such sorrowful emotions. He is unexpectedly drawn to her, intrigued by her spirit. But he shouldn't be.

"I have spent many a millennium determining the fates of souls," he starts, pushing through his discomfort. "It was the reason I was created. But…."

His slight hesitation has Marcy leaning forward, intrigued by his sudden caginess.

Masks that usually spin at a leisurely pace freeze as Asta admits, "You are my last judgment, Marcy."

Chapter 3

Astamesiophelous

Marcy presses her lips together, her face scrunched. Perhaps she fears that she is to blame for this being his final evaluation, but that is not the case.

"When I am at the end of my life cycle, I become one with the world, similar to you," Asta quickly clarifies, hoping to ease her distress. "But for beings like me, we are turned into stardust and aide in the creation of new universes."

"But you're not alive?" she questions, reaching to press against one of Asta's long flight feathers. She drags her fingers down the hollow shaft of the feather, gasping with joy at the texture once she reaches the bottom.

Asta shivers, and the rings around his head increase in their pace. He wishes for her to stroke his feathers again and maybe his chest too, or his rings…

I can't be thinking like this.

I'm…

"I'm becoming too human," he blurts, whipping his feathers back against his torso.

Marcy laughs humorlessly, her frown pained. "Why are you saying that like it's a bad thing?"

"It's not a bad thing," Asta asserts, waving his hands back and forth in denial. "Human emotions are lovely. You are complex creatures, experiencing a vast array of feelings such as elation, grief, or anger. Despite hardships, you love so fiercely, even if it means you may be hurt in the end. Please do not misunderstand me, Marcy. *I* do not believe humanity is an undesirable trait."

Asta's passionate torrent of words draw a deep blush to her face, spreading until the crimson hue disappears beneath the neckline of her dress.

Tucking her chin into her shoulder bashfully, Marcy asks, "But? I feel like there is a 'but' after that."

Shaking his rings, he is filled with disgrace as he admits, "My task, as the Evaluator, is to judge human souls *objectively,* to maintain complete indifference. I am forbidden to interfere with or experience any emotions, so as not to taint the evaluations with sympathy nor reproach. However, after spending millennia witnessing all facets of human life, whether it be horrifying or uplifting, I have, myself, begun to exhibit some human traits."

"Ah, and therefore, you can't remain objective," she replies, tapping her chin. "But didn't you say that you needed to 'feel' my emotions to understand me?"

"That is different," he says, staring out at the sun as it dips below the water's horizon. "When we witness your memories, I am nothing more than a conduit. Your emotions run through me to help me understand your thoughts and convictions, which makes evaluation easier."

Marcy snorts in amusement. "Is that so you can tell how I truly feel about a memory? If I'm actually remorseful or simply trying to trick you?"

"Precisely. But, as a side effect, the emotions can cling to me, festering until they become my own," he says, wings drooping in dismay.

"That's cruel," she says with a scowl.

"How so?"

"It doesn't seem right to rob you of your emotions the moment you begin to experience anything other than apathy."

"No, you do not understand. Ethereal beings don't feel emotion, and more importantly, we are not *allowed* to," Asta states, his voice booming. He does not intend to sound harsh, and he immediately regrets it when Marcy winces.

He continues but makes an effort to significantly lower his voice. "After I determine the fate of your soul, I will cease to exist. That is the way it is meant to be."

Marcy does not reply. Instead, she simply gazes at the ocean as it continues to creep further up the beach. A strong wave splashes past her feet and up her legs, making her tense from the sudden chill. She is stubborn enough to not move from her spot, but she turns her chest and shoulders away in discomfort.

I must never raise my voice at her again, he thinks. *She becomes so quiet and despondent when I do. I don't like it. I wish to see her smile.*

He scolds himself for his carelessness, disappointed that he accidentally hurt the only human to ever be friendly to him. Social interaction is not common in his evaluations, and when granted the opportunity for conversation, he was not often treated with decency. He cannot squander this opportunity, especially with someone as kind as Marcy.

"I know you do not want to relive another memory, but we must carry on," Asta says delicately as he places his hand on her shoulder. He strokes her skin through the fabric of her dress. She startles, snapping her attention to him. "There is still much to review, and I'm afraid that it is unlikely to get easier from here."

She didn't flinch at my touch this time.

Sighing with a slight whine, Marcy hangs her head. "Can it please be a good one?"

Chuckling, Asta opens his palm in a bid for her hand. "I don't get to decide that, unfortunately."

He worries she will refuse, given her withdrawal and current mood after his outburst. Readying an apology, he starts to retract his hand. To his surprise, unlike the previous times he offered it, she doesn't look frightened by his hand. She places her fingers on his wrist, then runs the pads along his palm until she reaches the center, enveloping her hand inside his.

His rings spin wildly. The dull heat of exhilaration blooms within him. While pleasant, it is also petrifying.

This is exactly the problem.

And why he needs to be turned into stardust.

Chapter 4

Marcy

Sharp blades of grass emerge beneath Marcy's feet, and the scent of falling leaves drifts through the crisp autumn air. A forest appears only a stone's throw away, with stacks of branches and raked leaves piled at the trees' edge.

Marcy gasps and crouches beside a collection of sticks. Her cheeks flush as she scans the fields around the tree line.

"This is… a good memory, no?" Asta asks hesitantly. He seems reserved in how he holds his hands at his chest, waiting for her approval.

A young woman approaches the forest before mirroring Marcy's crouched position by the sticks. She is carrying fruit and vegetable scraps in the skirt of her dress, and the linen fabric is stained red from strawberry tops.

Marcy glances between Asta and the young woman, a grin transforming her entire face.

"It's a wonderful memory, yes," she confirms. "During a particularly brutal harvest season, a wild bunny was injured by one of our cows. The poor thing fled to this heap of sticks to rest, and I took care of her until she was healthy enough to leave on her own."

Asta hums in acknowledgment, the melody carrying dulcet tones. He flies closer to the young woman, observing her as she places the scraps from her dress in a clearing between the pile of branches. The woman is joyous in her task, clapping her hands together once she's finished.

"The bunny would only come out to eat after I left, but sometimes she wouldn't mind my company," Marcy explains, giggling when the bunny's pink nose peeks out from the shadows. "There she is!"

Asta stares in amazement as the rabbit cautiously creeps out from her hiding spot, stretching her neck to take a bite from the core of a bell pepper. Her whiskers twitch as she chews, before she grows brave enough to approach the spinach leaves scattered near the young woman's feet.

The woman, whose hands are now excitedly clasped at her collarbone, begins to tear up. Not an ounce of sadness wells in her eyes, only a delicate shine of pure adoration.

"How beautiful," Asta whispers, seemingly to himself. "To take such loving care of a creature humanity deemed lesser is a testament to a kind heart." There is something akin to reverie woven through his tone, but Marcy can't place it.

It's peculiar to witness a faceless creature express such enthusiastic emotions, even though he claims he is not supposed to. He may not understand the feelings, given how he keeps turning his rings toward her to gauge her reaction, but he seems to feel safe expressing them around her.

It's endearing to see him look for my approval, she thinks happily.

This is the first time Marcy met a person — or rather, an ethereal being — who spoke to her with consideration, and it just happens to be in the moments before her soul is likely to be torn apart.

It's a tad ironic.

The young woman suddenly breaks into a sob, pulling Marcy away from her thoughts. The woman's hands cradle her stomach with clenched fingers. She falls to her side, curling into a fetal position.

"Why, God… why did you make me broken? What did I do?" she

cries, wiping her sniffling nose with the back of her hand. "He'll never love me if I'm damaged." Her chest trembles with each heaving sob, and she coughs as she chokes on her own tears.

Asta's hands and wings draw back in dismay.

"I-I thought this was a good memory," he frets, frantically swiping through the memory as if he were clearing a table covered in dust. "I'm so sorry."

He flinches when Marcy laughs, the sound of her cackles harmonizing with the young woman's wails.

"It's okay," Marcy says, pushing to her feet. She takes Asta's hand in her own, jerking her head toward the crying woman. "It's not *all* a bad memory, I assure you."

Asta gives her hand a gentle squeeze, a deep sigh in his chest. "If you insist."

Marcy's heart flutters as his water-like touch sparks across her skin, quickening her pulse.

They watch together, hand in hand, gawking at the woman who remains lying on the ground. She weeps until there are no tears left to stain her cheeks. It's then, in her silence, that the rabbit, who has been eating with glee, looks up from the scraps.

"Hello, little one," the young woman greets, snickering as the bunny's nose and ears wiggle in response. "Did you enjoy your food?"

The rabbit hops forward, tilting its head inquisitively at the young woman. Her injured hock lags as she sits upright, paws tucked to her chest as though in prayer.

The young woman and the animal sit inches apart, their eyes locked.

Marcy speaks in tandem with the woman, their voices echoing together.

"If only it were as easy for me as it is for you."

The bunny flees back into the pile of sticks before the memory begins to fade, and the woman gives an amused, hearty laugh.

"Until we meet again, little one," she calls out, smoothing the wrinkles in her dress and rising to her feet as their surroundings begin to distort.

Marcy looks down at where her and Asta's hands are still connected, then lifts her gaze to his rings. Her eyes crinkle with a smile as she says, "I guess I forgot about that last part, but this has always been a fond memory for me, overall. It was the first time a bunny approached me on their own and the closest I ever got to one."

"Are you partial to rabbits?" he asks.

She raises her brows for a split second. His interest in her preferences seems irrelevant to his evaluation, but she's not opposed to sharing pieces of herself. No one ever bothered to ask when she was alive. Even if this is some thinly veiled trick to get her to incriminate herself, she can't be bothered to care.

"They have a special place in my heart, yes. I adored feeding the wild ones, and some of them became accustomed to being around me. Feeding them was the only part of preparing dinner that I enjoyed," she says, motioning to tuck a nonexistent piece of hair behind her ear. "But it wasn't just the rabbits I tried to take care of."

Marcy always believed that all God's creatures deserved mercy and patience, no matter how small or unappealing. Asta's impressed reaction must be indicative of the rarity of such a trait, but she doesn't think it's anything out of the ordinary.

"With your permission, I'd like to see more," he says, readying his hand to push the memory forward. "But this won't count toward your evaluation, I'm afraid."

"That's alright. I think I'd like to see it, too," she says with a smile. Having a buffer between the upcoming bad memories would help her mental fortitude. That, and she'd love to see some cute animals to lift her spirits.

Memories rush by like a film played at thrice its normal speed. The blurred silhouette of the same woman shows her placing scraps and branches near the ever-growing woodpile. When the memory stops, the young woman is peering up into the trees, their branches hanging low from the weight of freshly fallen snow.

"Ah!" Marcy exclaims, pointing to the stilled image. "This was the year it snowed more than usual, so the blue jays in the forest struggled to eat. I snagged some peanuts from the bar my husband frequented to feed them."

Asta laughs gently at the handful of blue jays in the trees, all staring wishfully down at the young woman.

"They'd watch me through the windows, getting ready for the day, and wouldn't stop jeering at me until I tossed out food," she laughs alongside Asta, then points down at the pile of sticks. "Chickadees took up residence when the bunny moved out. When I initially approached them, they all burst out in a hurry and scared me half to death."

The memories press forward again, slowing when the woman approaches the tree line with her hands cupped. She squats, opening her fingers close to the grass. Looking a bit put off, she pulls her head and shoulders back as if shying away from a flame.

"Is she praying?" Asta asks, leaning his rings forward to look closer.

Marcy shakes her head, rubbing her neck bashfully. "No, I was releasing a spider. But I was always fearful of them."

After a few beats, the woman shoots up, flailing her hands wildly as she grimaces. She darts back toward the small house in the distance, repeatedly rubbing her hands on her apron.

"You don't like them, yet you help them?"

She shrugs, shooting him an incredulous look. "Well, yeah. They don't deserve to be killed because I don't like them. They're just trying to survive, like every other living being."

He hums, fingers dancing at the feathers below his rings as he says, "How fascinating."

"Is it that uncommon?" she prods.

"No, not at all," he supplies with a sigh. "But cruelty is easier than compassion, and humanity regularly chooses the former when it's against something they deplore. It's often those who are wounded the most who are capable of the deepest compassion — I find it tragic … yet comforting."

Marcy snorts humorlessly, pinching her lips together. She never entertained the notion that pain drove the human spirit to be brighter, that suffering was a prerequisite for empathy. It makes her wonder if she would ever exchange her compassionate nature for the chance of a fear-free life, where she'd never flinch from a loud noise.

"You look displeased," Asta whispers, stroking the back of her hand with his thumb.

Her face contorts, as if smelling something bad. "That all seems a little dramatic."

Resting his wing across her shoulders, he says, "One's true nature is shown in the actions taken with no one watching."

"Stop treating me like I'm some kind of saint," Marcy scoffs, rolling her eyes.

"I'm unsure why you view yourself so negatively. There is much goodness in you."

"If I were *actually* good, God would have allowed me to have children," she snaps. "My life would have been a lot different if I had been able to provide my husband with a son. Since I couldn't fulfill my purpose as a wife, I was punished for it."

"You may have been punished by humankind, but the gods are not so callous," he says with an edge of distress.

Hanging her head, Marcy lets out a pained groan. "It may be hard for you to understand, but there were expectations of me that I couldn't meet, no matter how much I wanted to. It's difficult not to think that God made me this way on purpose as retribution for my sins. Compassion for animals *or* humans will not absolve that."

Disdain and grief are woven into her voice, and her words fall apart as she swallows past the lump in her throat. "I don't even know why I deserve such a comprehensive judgment. God showed me what he thought of me during my lifetime. Why must I suffer through it again?"

"The gods do not care about such things as fertility. Humans were the source of your suffering, and that is a continued fault of humankind. The criterion for evaluation is different." Asta's words thunder. He doesn't notice how tightly he squeezes her palm while working himself up, his harsh grip accompanied by a light trembling. "We are nothing like the god you worshiped."

"That doesn't change the fact that I let down my loved ones. The memories don't show you how often I was drunk at church, or when I lied about breaking my husband's expensive watch. The horrible and cruel things I said about other ladies in the church group, even after we started fresh…." She huffs, her face turning red with guilt and anxiety. "And on top of all that, I was barren. My body betrayed me at the one thing it was supposed to be capable of. After I failed so many times, I couldn't allow my husband to touch me…."

Turning her gaze away but not pulling from Asta's grasp, her lip quivers as she says, "I was a failure as a wife, and I was a selfish person. Stop trying to paint me in a good light because I was kind every once in a while. I've always felt — *feel* — so…" She bites her lower lip, the words coming out sharp. "So *worthless*, so *useless*, so *ugly*—"

Marcy yelps when she's suddenly yanked forward, her cheeks pressed into downy feathers that envelop one side of her face. She feels hands press against her back, keeping her steady as Asta lifts her to his chest, rocking her in time with the beat of his wings.

"You are *nothing* of the sort," Asta says. The rumbling in his chest vibrates against her skull. "I felt the emotions passing through you during your memories, and I am certain you are nothing like the lies you believe about yourself."

His embrace is warm, evoking a deep, untroubled sigh from her. She never realized how much she needed this; how little she was held by anyone in her life.

He continues, stroking the top of her head like one would a skittish animal. "The memories aren't showing the things you spoke of because they are not an accurate judge of your character."

A somber smile pulls at her mouth, then her lips thin until no pink is visible. "You were able to conclude all of that from two memories?" she questions with heavy sarcasm.

Can he feel my emotions that *strongly? Enough to know what kind of person I am?*

Could he... understand me?

Asta's rings *clink* together as he shakes them. "All humans are flawed; it is a part of living. Making mistakes does not make you evil, even if they are harmful. You are not your worst moments, Marcy. You possess a beauty in both appearance and nature that can make even a cold, cruel being like myself understand the breadth of your compassion. Do not think so disparagingly about yourself. Please."

Her eyebrows lift to her hairline. She's stunned not only by the conviction of his words but also by his firm, yet comforting, hug. He holds her like a giant would a small bird, as if she *means* something to him.

"I apologize if I said something insensitive," he mutters above her ear. "My blossoming emotions do not equate to emotional intelligence."

She can't help but snicker, burrowing her face deeper into his breast.

Marcy has never been partial to physical touch, but for some reason, with Asta, she doesn't seem to mind. It feels natural, easy, as though anywhere but his arms would be abnormal or foreign.

A sudden heat radiates throughout her body, a feeling she thought was long lost, bubbling to the surface. The cinders that burn at her core feel hot enough to light Asta's feathers on fire.

What is wrong with me?

The unexpected blossoming of such unsolicited desire for a creature like Asta confuses her. It makes her feel pathetic that such a simple act of tenderness can elicit such a physical response, but she isn't compelled to ignore it. If anything, she wants to cultivate it. To encourage Asta to speak to her gently, to have him describe every trait he finds pleasing in her with ardor and make her lower abdomen pool with more warmth.

Being around him…. makes Marcy hate herself a little less.

Becoming nervous from his touch and subsequent flustering emotions, Marcy inadvertently tenses.

Asta pulls away when he senses her discomfort. "I'm sorry. Did I scare you? I didn't mean to be so forthright. I understand that it can be distressing, coming from someone with my appearance. I can change into a human form, if that would be more pleasing," he says, dejected.

Marcy smirks, breathing in his delicate, vanilla aroma.

Here I am startled by the attraction I feel, and he's anxious over keeping my favor.

He's like a puppy. Easy to upset, quick to excite.

"I meant what I said before: I'd prefer it if you stayed like this," she assures him, wrapping her arms around the feathered base of his neck. "I like the way you look. I was just taken aback, is all."

She won't say it aloud, but she's grown to find Asta's form attractive. He's breathtaking, magnificent, and commanding, all at the same time. While the multiple eyes lining his wings were unsettling at first, his gaze now makes her cheeks flush, their attention seemingly always on her.

Asta's chest puffs with elation as Marcy absentmindedly plays with his feathers. "I've… yet to have a human prefer me this way, so it is hard for me to understand. Forgive me for my insistence, I don't want to scare you."

The innocent worry in his voice melts her heart, and she burrows her cheek into his soothing feathers. "You are like no man I've ever met."

"I'm not a man," Asta deadpans.

Marcy chuckles, a grin brightening her face. "Of course not. How silly of me," she says, lifting her chin to meet one of the many staring eyes on his wings. A spark of an idea flashes across her expression, and she asks, "I have a question for you: can you taste?"

The rings of his head cock to the side with unmistakable confusion. "If I will it to be, then yes."

"Okay," she begins, excitedly swaying against him. "Then take me to a memory inside my old home. There is something I want to show you."

Chapter 5

Astamesiophelous

The gods would be furious with him.

As the Evaluator, it is frowned upon to visit human memories upon request. His purpose is only to understand the human's soul, not to allow them to reminisce about their mortal life.

He tries to be dutiful when it comes to following the ethereal rules, but he is beginning to find it difficult to deny anything to this particular human. It may go against his orders, but he decides it's harmless to allow her to cook in the kitchen of her old home. Or rather, that is what he convinces himself to be true.

"Have you ever tasted anything before?" she asks, eagerly tying a pink floral apron around her waist. There are multicolored chickens stitched along the bottom hem, which match the hue of the straps tied just above her belly button.

She fastens the apron tightly, her curves spilling out against the ties like the bulge of freshly baked bread.

Gods, her waist.

"Asta?"

Jolting, Asta collects himself quickly enough to reply with minimal stammering. "Yes, but it was long ago. I don't recall."

Maybe if a beautiful woman offered to feed me before now, I would have.

He nearly snaps the table with his tight grip, frightened by the intrusion of such a lascivious thought.

The recent accumulation of human emotions brewing inside him never resulted in such a lewd response, particularly when said emotions were not lewd to begin with. There's an edge to these feelings, as though opening himself to Marcy's soul has altered his very being. None of this was helped by the way she hugged him, beaming as she teased his feathers.

Lifting his gaze to the kitchen, he dampens the acute terror caused by his thoughts before it can take permanent hold.

Assembling pots, pans, and ingredients from the fridge, Marcy is completely at ease among what Asta would consider a mess. She does not hesitate to start baking, cracking eggs skillfully into a bowl, all while not spilling a drop.

He watches her intently, the grace in her movements akin to that of the beings who waltz across the clouds in the ethereal realm. None of them, however, could maneuver around a kitchen, doing whatever it is she is doing, with as much passion and joy.

"I'm going to make you my favorite pie: apple," she declares, peeling the skin off a plump, red fruit with a small knife. The pads of her fingertips are lined with minor cuts, most of them scarred and healed over. She must not have always been skillful with a knife.

"My husband liked them with Granny Smiths, but I prefer Honeycrisp. I like the sweetness," she says with a wink.

An unfamiliar feeling claws its way into Asta's chest. Something adjacent to *human want.* Not in a fulfilling way, but rather, in a satiating way.

Selfish.

In all his millennia of existence, Asta has never wanted anything. No ethereal being does. He has never felt hunger, thirst, or a need for gratification. Anything he could ever need is immediately fulfilled by his will alone. But now, there exists a primal urge, a covetous desire, to steal Marcy away for himself.

Is it selfish? To want someone's satisfaction so badly?

She hums a tune, and her plump lips are wet with juice as she sneaks a few bites of apple for herself. She lays a lattice of pastry atop the pie, then brushes a watery egg mixture over it. After she places the pie in the oven, she wipes her flour-covered palms against her apron.

Whirling around, she turns the dial on a timer that sits on the counter.

She smirks at Asta, playfully waggling her brows. "You can't magically make the pie cook quicker, can you?"

"No," he replies. In truth, he's unsure if he would be able to influence anything so detached from a memory. But he'd rather not find out, fearful he may succeed.

She purses her lips in a teasing pout as she slides into the kitchen chair next to his. "Well, that's too bad. I'm anxious to hear what an angel thinks of my baking. It's my own recipe, and I'm quite proud of it."

She is strangely interested in my opinion.

Not that he minds.

As Marcy leans back in her chair, Asta finds himself painfully aware of her every move.

"I'm certain it's lovely," he assures, turning his attention away so as not to ogle.

Tucking his wings, Asta is careful not to bump the various dirty dishes stacked along the counter. While he's unable to *sit* by definition, he can place himself through a chair to appear as such.

"It's weird to think that this is the last time I'll bake — or eat — this pie," Marcy muses, lolling her head to the side.

He chuckles, reaching to brush the mussed hair from her sweat-dampened forehead.

"It'll be my last time, too."

Face alight, Marcy gasps as she exclaims, "It is, isn't it? First in a millennium as well as the last."

Humming, his touch lingers along her jaw, reveling in the softness of her velvety skin.

"I'm grateful we can experience it together."

A pink flush spreads across Marcy's cheeks, the rosy color illuminating the warm tones in her irises. It's as if her deep brown eyes are a momentary window into the loveliness of her soul.

"A human has never offered me food. This is a true first," Asta says, pulling his hand away. He fears that if he touches her any longer, he may act on his emotions and scare her.

Marcy shrugs and absentmindedly presses her fingers to the empty space Asta's touch left behind. She rubs her feet together beneath the table and tucks her chin into her chest. "I don't see how anyone could *not* be curious about what an angel thinks of their cooking. Especially when at the end of their life."

"Most humans are only concerned about their own lives during the evaluation; they don't waste time posing questions about me," he replies, the words harsher than he intended.

His tone doesn't faze Marcy. She frowns and says, "What a horrible lack of curiosity. To meet an angel and not ask them anything? Humans are disgraceful."

At first, he worries that she is angry, but a slight crack in her composure reveals that she is teasing him. Asta laughs, delighted by her uplifted mood.

He has never been teased before.

So many firsts.

Shaking her leg beneath the table, she rests her chin in her palm and gives him a smile.

She is a different person when she is cheerful. Even more beautiful.

"So, what do you do for fun when you aren't evaluating souls? Visit with angel friends or something?" Marcy asks.

The question is so absurd he nearly laughs again, but the gentle pinch in her forehead suggests she is being serious.

"No. We do not have friends, only tasks."

Saying it out loud makes it sound worse than it is. He is one of the few ethereal beings capable of experiencing emotions in the first place, so there is hardly an opportunity to make a genuine connection with the others.

She grimaces and juts out her lower lip. "How lonely."

It is.

With each evaluation, the loneliness sinks deeper. Time and time again, he watches the memories of humans falling in love, creating families, and forging meaningful relationships with one another. All things he has not, and never will, be able to experience.

The humans he evaluates never try to form a friendship with him, even though they are the only ones capable of it. Instead, he is often treated with disdain, and sometimes hatred. But that is the reality he was created to bear.

His hands fiddle with one another, unsure what to do with them. "The other ethereal beings can't experience emotions, so it's pointless to seek comfort from them," he says quietly. "But it does not matter anyway, since my evaluations leave little room for fraternization, of any form."

Marcy's expression remains troubled, her shoulders drooping with an exhale.

He scolds himself for answering her question in such morose terms, no matter how accurate it may be. He tries desperately to think of another topic, specifically one that will alleviate her dismay.

Thankfully, Marcy beats him to it. "Do you have a favorite memory that you've witnessed?" she asks, drumming her fingers on the table.

More questions about me.

"I particularly enjoy memories about mortals falling in love," he replies, turning his gaze to the oven. "Oftentimes, it's complicated, but there is nothing sweeter than burgeoning love. The emotions are… addicting."

There is no eloquent way to explain it. Any time he becomes the vessel for emotions where there is even a *shred* of affection, the pit of solitude rotting his essence subsides.

"How adorable," Marcy says sweetly. "I didn't think you'd be the romantic type."

Her flattering words cause him to ruffle his feathers with pride.

The timer on the counter rings, and Marcy shoots up from her chair. She rushes to the oven with a bounce in her step and pulls the piping-hot pastry out before placing it onto a cooling mat.

After clattering through more dishes, she sets a plate full of steaming apple pie in front of Asta before jabbing a fork through the lattice top.

"Go on, try it!" she urges so jovially that the corners of her eyes wrinkle with her smile.

Not one to refuse her enthusiasm, Asta lifts the entire slice of gooey, sweet-smelling pie and shoves it into the seam of his chest, the only part of his body that can accept matter. Marcy seems surprised by the sudden gesture, but it doesn't seem to sicken her as it has for other mortals.

The flavors explode inside him. Syrupy apples blend with the crisp pastry topping, and a touch of sour cuts through the sweetness. Hints of cinnamon, clove, and other warming spices captivate his senses, as if a small fire was lit at the base of his chest. It burns, but in a good way.

Before he can craft an assessment, he notices Marcy press the pads of her fingers to her bottom lip, trying to curtail her uncontrollable giggles.

"I haven't told you what I thought, yet?" he questions.

She points a finger at the rings of his head. "You don't have to. Your rings started spinning like a toy top the moment you took a bite."

Embarrassment floods his torso and wings, making his eyes go wide. He's impressed she was able to ascertain that his rings display his mood, a feature most humans overlook. That means she has been paying attention to him.

"My little lamb, it is a marvel," he says, placing his fork back onto the empty plate. "Truly divine. I'm more than honored to have experienced it as my last taste of food."

"That's quite the praise," she chortles, looking slightly self-conscious. She digs into her own piece of pie, stuffing her mouth until she can barely close it. "I can't get full, right? Because I intend to eat that entire pie."

His hands twitch, desperate to cup her fat, round cheeks. "Eat as much as you like."

If he were guaranteed moments like this, then maybe Asta wouldn't mind the agony of human emotions. But only if Marcy were there with him, laughing in the boisterous way she does. He would never tire of the way she lifts her brows when she's curious about something, but is embarrassed to ask, and how she smiles with her entire heart, not caring if it causes wrinkles. Each gorgeous line on her face is rightfully deserved.

In the past, he would normally feel ashamed by these thoughts. Instead, he is now overcome with longing and a feeling of fullness caused by something other than her pie.

Perhaps, this is what it feels like to fall in love. To have kinship.

If he could experience humanity with Marcy, then maybe, for the first time, he would be satiated.

Chapter 6

Marcy

"How many memories do we have left?" Marcy asks as she closes the door to her old home.

Their surroundings turn to mist before recollecting into the blurry interior of another building. Marcy can't make out where they're supposed to be as the walls shoot up from the ground to form a tight corridor.

The change of scenery is disorienting, and she reaches for Asta's hand to keep herself stable as nausea causes her skin to flush. Her fingers slip between his with ease, his palm large and inviting.

He squeezes her hand and tips his rings to look at her.

"I'm unsure of how many there are left to witness. The gods do not keep me privy to that information, but I have an inclination that we are nearing the end," he replies, using his free hand to sharpen the hazy tableau. "There are many details missing from this memory, but I will do my best to fill in the blanks. I apologize if any of it is incorrect."

If it's something Marcy doesn't remember, she doubts she would be able to tell if anything is changed in the first place. She normally has a keen eye and a retentive memory, so this must be from her early childhood. Or so she hopes.

An ugly pattern swirls along the floor as the scene takes shape, revealing dirty carpeting illuminated by fluorescent lighting. The walls are busy with gaudy wallpaper and photos of generic landscapes, which interrupt the multitude of doors cascading down an unending hallway.

Marcy's stomach drops, and a cold sweat beads at the back of her neck as the sinews stand on end. A sense of recognition tingles in her brain, but there's a stinging pain that prevents her from bringing any clarity to this memory.

This is...

The hallway doors are identical to each other, except for the iron lettering above their peepholes. The door in front of them reads: *Room 213.*

Tugging from Asta's soft grip, Marcy darts down the hallway with breakneck speed. Her mouth hangs open as she pants, not from exertion, but from panic. It feels like her rapidly beating heart is about to puncture a hole straight through her chest.

I have to get out.

The hallway is endless, with no stairwell or windows in sight. But that doesn't matter; Marcy keeps running.

It's only when she smacks into a familiar plume of feathers that she is forced to stop, falling onto her bottom. Her vision is bleary with tears, and her voice comes out in a hollowing scream.

"I won't go in that room! You can't make me!"

Asta lowers himself to her level, and the rings hovering above his wings drift behind her. From out of those rings, he forms another pair of hands, which gently slide beneath her armpits to help lift her from the dingy carpet.

"It will be difficult, I know, little—"

"No!" she screams, slapping him away. "I *refuse*. I'd rather spend the rest of my afterlife trapped in the hallway of this disgusting hotel."

Hurt flashes in Asta's eyes, but Marcy can't bring herself to feel bad. He'll never understand such a *human* situation, no matter how many new emotions — how much empathy — he has. Forcing her to relive this night is cruelty beyond comprehension.

While she knew she'd have to witness distressing moments, she never expected to relive this particular memory. Just the thought of opening that hotel room door makes her sick to her stomach. Any sense of jubilation that lingered from sharing her pie with Asta is long gone.

"You. Can't. Make. Me," she reiterates, curling her upper lip.

She expects Asta to repeat the same words from before, explaining that she has no choice. To force her to experience this moment as she has the others, simply because it's the "rules" of the evaluation, ignoring her discomfort.

But instead, he says something unexpected.

The arms protruding from Asta's rings cup beneath where her shoulders connect to her biceps. Low and mellifluous, as if coaxing a child, he says, "I won't make you, if that is your request."

"R-really?" she stammers. Her breathing immediately slows, the hot brand of panic easing from such a simple sentence.

He lifts a knuckle and brushes it along her cheekbone. "I will not. So please, do not cry."

She has lost control over the flow of her tears, but she makes an effort to look a little less miserable.

"Okay," she says, forcing a slight smile.

Asta's rings wobble.

"If we are not able to witness this memory, can you tell me what happened?" He is careful with his language but still stares at her with an invasive curiosity that she'd expect from a human, not a being such as him.

Allowing herself to be lifted to her feet, Marcy draws her arms to her chest, cradling her elbows. "I don't want to talk about it. *See* it, *think* about it — I never want to remember anything from that night. I don't think…" She sucks in a deep breath, her brows tightly furrowed. "I don't think I would be able to survive it a second time."

The tears she tried so hard to stifle slide down her cheeks and chin, and the cross on her necklace *clinks* against the buttons of her dress as she hiccups. The moisture burns her cheeks, and her eyelids are raw and puffy. She's beyond tired of crying, of feeling sorrow for a version of herself that she wishes she could protect. A version she let down.

"Marcy?" he calls in a whisper.

Blinking away the tears, she looks up at Asta, who is no longer crouching in front of her. He stands fully upright, arms extended in invitation.

She doesn't need an explanation to understand his intention. Poking at the arms hovering idly by her side, she wordlessly consents to be lifted into his waiting embrace.

Snaking her hands around his fluffy body, she shamelessly nuzzles her face into his neck. The sadness and anger ripping her heart to pieces immediately calms as she sinks further into his soothing warmth.

Asta curls his fingers around her waist, cocooning his wings around both of them to silence the buzzing of overhead lights.

"I will not make you go through that door. Okay?" he murmurs, sliding a hand up the length of her spine to cradle the back of her head. He nestles her closer, and the rise and fall of his chest soon matches time with her own.

He smells so lovely, she thinks, inhaling deeply through her nose. *It's not just vanilla. It's something else too.* Goosebumps rise over her skin as she takes another breath.

"Asta," Marcy starts, unable to raise her eyes from his chest. "What happened behind that door is one of the worst moments of my entire life. It's not only that I never wish to relive it, but it's also that I… I don't want *you* to see me like that."

A moment of silent cognizance passes between them, but Marcy still fears he will make her press on. He hasn't told her what he already knows about her or if he was given any context for the memories before witnessing them.

For this memory, he'll want to know more. Everyone always does. Her heart sinks, squeezing like a vice until it's ready to pop.

To her surprise, he remains silent. He seems unsure of how to comfort her, but he still tries.

He strokes the small of her back with his thumb, and the gentle beat of his lower wings rocks them softly. Marcy may not want him to see the worst moments of her life, but there is a part of her that still wants him to know *her*. She wants him to know the pieces of herself that are missing, the ones that have been irreparably broken.

Would he still hold me in high regard?

Tightly pursing her lips together in abhorrence, she nervously twirls a stray hair at the nape of her neck. "It's my wedding night," she confesses.

Asta seems to struggle with his next words, as dictated by the noises he makes from starting and stopping his sentence. Maybe he is deciding if it's more important to follow his duty or to indulge her pitiful request. She hopes it's the latter.

"I…." his voice is hoarse, sounding so uncannily human it's startling. "It's okay. You need not explain anything further. I will not make you speak of it again. I promise." The last words are an oath, meant to show how much he truly means them.

"Thank you, Asta," she says, pressing herself tighter against him.

Anxiety trickles through her, down her spine to her feet. She is vulnerable, flayed open until she is completely bare. It doesn't matter that she is standing in the same hallway where the greatest horrors of her life took place, where she vowed she would never fully give herself to anyone.

For some unknown reason, when she is with Asta, the constant tempest of insecurity and animosity she felt toward herself her entire life starts to quell. The hallway seems to fade away, and the fuchsia streaks of a peaceful sky brought on by Asta's warmth finally shine through the clouds.

Oh, how warm the sun feels against her cheek.

Despite her better judgment, she confesses a shameful secret that has been on her mind. If she doesn't say it now, she fears she will never have the courage.

"I've never been touched so tenderly before," she admits while rubbing his smaller down feathers. "I've never craved holding someone else's hand in my own or feeling their arms around my waist. I've certainly never allowed it willingly, at least not without the terror that I'll end up being hurt."

He brightens, his rings spinning faster.

"You enjoy when I touch you?" he questions, flabbergasted.

His obvious excitement at that knowledge flusters Marcy to a point of near combustion. Asta's blunt way of speaking is far too much for her fragile heart, but then again, it's a piece of him that she's quickly coming to adore.

Scraping her nails along his sides, she nods against his chest. "I do. I enjoy it a lot."

It makes me feel safe.

"That is another first for me," he says with genuine surprise and awe.

Marcy laughs, her shoulders shaking against him. "A woman could get used to this. It's not fair that I'll have to leave you so soon."

If she could choose, she would spend her entire afterlife here with Asta. She knows it's impossible, but, if only for a moment, she'd like to pretend that she could.

"Then," he hesitates, self-conscious, but he continues anyway, "why don't we explore another good memory? Something we can experience together."

Together.

How wonderful having a 'together' feels.

She kicks her feet with excitement as a smile pulls at her lips. "Oh! I know exactly which memory," she exclaims. "But wait — is there a limit to how large an area you can create?"

"No. Request anything, and I will make it so."

Her heart flutters.

Gazing up at him through her lashes, she asks, "It'll be crowded, so you'll hold my hand the entire time, right?"

A surprised gasp bursts out of him like a popped balloon, and for the first time, Marcy recognizes his emotion as anxiety. "I… I will embrace you whenever you like, Marcy. From now until the last moments when we part," he mutters, his confidence wobbling. If he was capable of it, she would swear he was blushing.

He's as nervous as a teenager on his first date.

Well, it *is* a first date, in a way. At least, she'd like to think so. Even if it is a bad idea, something that might shatter her in the end, one little outing couldn't hurt. Could it?

Chapter 7

Astamesiophelous

With a snap of his fingers, he commands the energy of the ethereal realm to scour Marcy's memories for the time and location she describes. Asta vibrates with excitement, and his many eyes widen to take in the environment before it materializes around them.

Green, prickly trees pop up in neat rows along a brick road. Everything is dusted in white powder. Hanging lights are strung between the tallest trees, crisscrossing over a crowded street that echoes with jovial laughter and conversation. A band plays upbeat music, and there is the distinct sound of bells incorporated into the harmony.

This scene is a stark contrast to the previous one, and the difference feels shocking. Noticing the chill in the air and the frozen flakes sticking to the sopping-wet ground, Asta materializes a small pair of heels in his palm.

Sensations like hot and cold are not felt as vividly in memories, but Asta would rather err on the side of caution, knowing how adverse Marcy is to making a fuss.

"These will help keep the snow off your feet. Here, take a seat," he says, motioning to a bench on the edge of the sidewalk.

She snorts, reluctant to accept his care. "Asta, it's fine. Don't —"

"I'm not asking," he says, a bit teasingly. It's clear he's serious, but he doesn't want to seem brutish.

Eyes widening, she falls to the bench as instructed. "I didn't take you to be such a stickler for safety, since you've been so lenient about *other* rules," she says pointedly, balling her hands in her lap.

He panics at first, not expecting her to be upset about his flippant rule violations. Her wry smirk, on the other hand, tells a different tale.

"I am concerned about your comfort. If you are *that* opposed, then consider wearing them for my benefit," he says, lifting her foot by the heel.

His fingers brush over the top of her foot, the delicate skin twitching as her whole body shudders. She's ticklish, which he finds charming.

"Fine, if it'll make you happy. But why these shoes in particular?"

The answer is obvious: they are the only pair her husband never saw her wear. To be more specific, they are the only pair she purchased of her own volition, not guided by a heavy hand. Her husband favored her in beige and neutral tones, regardless of her preference.

The shoes Asta chose from her memories are much louder in style, with button clasps, a multitude of straps, and bright patterns. They match her vibrant personality more than any of the others she owned.

They also bring her joy, as evidenced by her bright expression, which makes him love them too.

"I just think they are fun," he replies. Not a total lie, but the truth is irrelevant.

She hums skeptically, clearly not buying his explanation. But she doesn't press.

Placing her foot within the shoe, he tightens the buckle before securing it in place. He taps the calf of her other leg, and she wiggles in response, squeezing her thighs together.

Marcy grips the skirt of her dress the entire time he is crouched before her. It's an act that seems benign, yet electricity crackles between them whenever his fingers accidentally graze her skin. Well, not every touch is *completely* accidental.

Once both shoes are secure, she looks down and clicks her heels together playfully.

"Thank you," she mumbles before standing and smoothing the creases from her dress. She stares at the ground, like she's intentionally avoiding eye contact, and keeps her gaze on the surroundings that are slowly slipping into focus.

The scene around them finally stabilizes. Such a large environment is difficult for Asta to recreate perfectly, but he'd hate for any of it to be inaccurate.

"Is this what you were imagining?" he asks, gesturing broadly.

She looks up with squinted, critical eyes, and her mouth falls agape. Her face lights up, and within seconds, she is bouncing up and down as she clutches the gold cross around her neck.

"Oh my goodness! It's just like the winter festival!" Marcy exclaims, her sparkling doe eyes deepening to a lovely shade of caramel as her pupils spread into black pools. A hint of underlying embarrassment lurks beneath her glee; perhaps she thinks her behavior is immature or childish, but she doesn't allow it to weaken her wide smile.

Using a ring and its resulting hand, he intertwines his fingers with hers. The way she squeezes his palm tightly makes his feathers rouse.

"We can do anything you want, little lamb." He's careful not to remind her of their finite time together, not wanting to spoil her joy.

Marcy presses her index and middle fingers to her bottom lip, forehead wrinkled in thought. She perks up with excitement as she says, "You *have* to try the church's homemade apple crisp — oh! And their hot cocoa! Then the midnight dance, and maybe the fireworks..." She trails off, swiveling her head to take in everything around them.

Asta chuckles.

I made all this for her, yet she remains considerate of me.

The arm attached to his torso gently presses the small of her back. "We won't miss a thing. Say the word, and I'll make it appear. Alright?"

Nodding furiously, Marcy bites down on her lip, her cheeks puffing. She presses closer to Asta, tucking herself under his wings.

His insides nearly burst with joy from her proximity. If he had a heart, it would surely be palpitating.

"Let's try the food first," she suggests, looking up at him shyly. "If that's okay with you?"

A rumbling laugh vibrates from his chest, and Marcy's eyes go wide. The spark of dejection that crosses her face does not go unnoticed. She thinks he is making fun of her.

"You needn't ask my permission, Marcy," he quickly amends. "I am delighted to do whatever it is you please, so long as we can do it together."

The subtle fear in her timid expression subsides, and her inviting smile soon returns. She lifts their laced hands to her mouth, gently brushing her lips over his knuckles.

Soft.

Warm.

Wet.

I want to kiss her.

A tingling sensation zaps up his body and through each pair of his wings, causing the rings of his head to spiral at a dizzying speed. It takes every ounce of Asta's self-control to suppress a shudder and a more-than-uncouth moan.

"Then I want to get some sweets," she whispers bashfully against his skin, twirling the skirt of her dress with her opposite hand.

Asta beckons her to lead the way with his wings, which is the only cue she needs to dart directly for the pastry stand. Dragging him behind her, she cuts through the crowd with bubbly laughter.

"You certainly seem to know where to go," he observes as Marcy weaves around obstacles with laser-like focus.

She shrugs, brushing away the stray hairs that stick to the sides of her mouth. "I used to come here every year. It was one of the few events I looked forward to. I was free to have as much fun as I wanted, without ridicule or worrying about keeping up appearances," she explains. Her words are sullen in nature, but her tone would suggest otherwise.

They reach a petite wooden stand at the base of a towering, gaudy church, and Marcy doesn't hesitate to snag a plateful of sweets and a paper cup filled with a steaming, dark brown liquid.

She holds them out to Asta with the same excitement she had when sharing her homemade dessert.

"It's not apple pie, but apple crisp is somewhat similar," she says gleefully, grabbing a plate and cup for herself after Asta accepts the ones she gave him.

Inserting the apple crisp, plate and all, into the seam of his chest, he quickly realizes that it pales in every way compared to Marcy's pie. Then again, he's only consumed two foods in the last hundred millennia, including this one, so he decides it's best to reserve his judgment, especially given the way Marcy is anxiously awaiting his response.

"It's good," Asta says blandly, tipping his cup toward her. "However, I think your apple treat was much more enjoyable."

Marcy pauses as she lifts her fork to her mouth, biting back a modest, if proud, smile.

"That makes me happy to hear," she whispers.

Throwing the entire cup of hot liquid into his chest, Asta recoils as soon as he comprehends the taste.

Raising an eyebrow, Marcy scrapes her plate clean as she asks, "Don't like hot chocolate?"

Shaking his rings, he wipes the remaining residue from the liquid off his feathers.

"It's too sweet."

He scans her face, worried his opposing opinion might elicit a negative reaction. Thankfully, he's delighted to hear her snickering instead. She downs her drink in a single gulp, then tosses her plate and cup into an aluminum trash can.

"If I could, I'd take you to every restaurant in town until we discovered your favorite food," she says, snatching his hand. "But I'll just have to settle for showing you around the festival."

Asta's insides swirl with apprehension as Marcy pulls him toward the center of activity, her heels clicking on the stone path with each step. Up ahead, couples dance to fast-paced music under a canopy, which is hung over the make-shift dance floor to thwart the intrusion of snow. Each couple is red-faced, dancing vigorously despite their exhausted postures.

Watching the crowd, he is unsure what Marcy expects from him. He has no legs and therefore cannot replicate the movements of the human men who lift and swing their female partners. He is strung with a sense of inadequacy, and for a moment, he wishes she would ask him to appear human.

Marcy suddenly stops before they reach the dancers, her attention snagged by a stand covered with flashing lights. A brightly dressed man leans against a post at the front of the stand, holding three white balls.

Jutting her thumb toward the stand, she asks, "Have you ever played a carnival game before?"

"No," Asta replies. He's never danced, played a game, nor taken part in any of the activities this festival offers. Every bit of this is new to him, and the last thing he wants is to disappoint Marcy or make a fool of himself in front of her.

Marcy yanks him closer to the display, and he notices bottles stacked in the shape of a triangle. She lifts one of the white balls before comically winding up her arm.

"To win a prize, you have to knock down all three bottles," she explains, jerking her head in the direction of the stacked items. "Make sense?"

Asta watches observantly, a little confused as to the point of such a thing, but he does not voice the thought aloud.

Stepping forward while swinging her arm, Marcy throws a ball at the bottles, but she misses them entirely. The ball smacks against the canvas curtain behind the rows of hanging prizes before falling to the ground.

She scratches at the back of her neck, her lips pulled into a thin, disappointed line.

"I, uh, was never very good at these festival games," Marcy admits, leaning against the table in defeat. "My husband usually won the prizes for me."

Her husband.

Something about those words makes him irrationally angry. Anger is not something he often experiences, even with his own ever-increasing human emotions, but now it seems to take over his entire being, until he is seething.

"Was he good at this game?" Asta asks, desperately attempting to appear calm.

Marcy doesn't seem to notice his quiet, molten rage. She replies with a simple, "The best."

Wasting no time, Asta slips beside Marcy to grab one of the white balls.

"Oh, are you gonna try—"

The words barely leave her mouth before Asta throws his entire strength into toppling those three, simple bottles.

Her husband.

The words irk him. He dislikes feeling inferior, especially when compared to a human man.

That human man.

Pivoting his arm, Asta releases his throw.

The ball disappears for a split second, then reappears directly in front of the bottles, bursting them from inside out. A *crack* shakes the wooden stand, and the sound of impact is accompanied by a bright, blinding light. Pieces explode from the collision and disintegrate in the air before they reach the ground.

Turning to Marcy for approval, he instead sees that her eyebrows are hiked up to her hairline.

"Was that... not good?" Asta frets, unsure if he has unintentionally scared her. Or more importantly, lost the game.

His rings spin, flustered, and he self-consciously tucks his wings into his chest.

Marcy's lips part, then close, then open again into a slight smile. "No, that was... That was *very* good."

"Better than your husband?" It comes out instantly, but he's powerless to stop the question.

She cocks her head, snorting a laugh that doesn't reach her eyes. "There isn't a single trace of those bottles left, Asta. So yes, I'd say you're better than anyone else on earth."

His chest puffs with ego, delighted by her compliment.

"I didn't think you'd be so into it," she says, kicking off the post she is leaning against. "You don't seem to be the type."

He's not.

"I wanted to impress you."

Marcy's cheeks flush to a tantalizing cherry color, taken aback by his honest response. She curls an arm around his bicep, pressing her cheek into his chilled skin.

"Consider me impressed," she says, merrily running her fingers over his forearm.

Any response he had dies in his non-existent throat, Marcy's touch stealing his ability to think. Then come the nerves, stirring and coiling within him like a tornado.

"We win a prize, correct?" he chokes out, his voice cracking on the last syllable.

"Yeah, you can pick out anything you want," she says, the apples of her cheeks plump from her bright smile.

Most of the plush animals hanging from the prize rack are blurry from lack of memory, but a few are as clear as a summer sky.

At some point, her husband must have won those prizes for her. That's why she remembers them.

With that thought, he decides that none of them are adequate.

Reaching out to the prize rack, he creates a new stuffed animal that is visibly different from the others around it. He pulls it down and holds it out to Marcy.

"A bunny!" she exclaims in awe, pulling the animal to her chest and giving it a big squeeze. She cradles the plush in her arms, squealing with joy.

Although the stuffed toy is an incredibly adorable sight, Asta can not keep his attention off Marcy. It was difficult enough not to stare at her while she licked her fork clean, but this is one visual he can't resist.

In general, humans rarely excite him. Most are compelled to act in their own self-interest, which is to be expected when they realize they are dead and about to face judgment. Their intentions are often rooted in selfish gains. Very few break from that mold, making it rare for Asta to be surprised by their actions or behavior.

Marcy doesn't deviate from most norms: she is as flawed as any human Asta evaluated before her. But unlike the others, she doesn't see Asta as a monster, a terrifying and awe-striking creature depicted in biblical scripture or used as a frightening beast in a bedtime story. Despite his appearance, she treats him like any human she might meet, and *that* is what excites him.

To her, he is not just the Evaluator, an ethereal being plagued by budding human emotions. He is simply Astamesiophelous, a sentimental 'angel' who enjoys the apple sweets she makes him.

Setting the rabbit plush on the carnival stand's platform, Marcy grins sheepishly. "I can't exactly carry this around the rest of the night," she says, hooking her arm through his once again. "Especially since I want to dance."

"You do?" he asks, curious that someone as shy as her would wish to participate in such a public event.

"I never had the opportunity when I was alive. Can we dance? Please?" she asks, gently tugging Asta in the direction of the dance floor.

Asta relents, despite his reservations, and allows her to pull him toward the resonating music.

"I have never danced before, and I don't imagine I will be very good without a body or legs," he says as Marcy parts the sea of dancing humans, securing them ample space.

She needn't worry about his large wings and their potential to harm others, since the humans around them are not real. He admires her concern though, and the polite way she says, "Excuse me," to the blurry-faced crowd.

Once they reach the middle of the dance floor, Marcy shakes her head at him. "I can't dance, either. But we'll try anyway, okay?" she says with a laugh.

Looking down at his tail feathers, which are pooling on the stones below them, he tilts his rings. "What is it that I am supposed to do?"

Her eyes glint beneath the overhead lights, smirking deviously. "How about this: I'll lead, and you follow."

"I do not understand what that means."

Taking his hands in her own, she says, "I'll show you."

Squaring her posture while pushing out her chest, she places one of Asta's hands on her hip and the other in her outstretched right hand.

His entire hand could fit around Marcy's waist, consuming her in his grasp if he so wished. Her soft curves and wide hips provide the perfect place to rest his palm but make him curious as to what lies beneath the fabric of her dress.

Her thighs might also be squishy and plump. Like her pink lips, framing her uninhibited smile and—

"Move to your right — ah, sorry — *your* left, *my* right. Like this," Marcy instructs, interrupting his less-than-pure musings.

This time, however, he does not shy away from those thoughts.

Asta's developing desire is not helped by the sway of her body against his palm or her boisterous giggling. It is an addictive sound he never thought he'd hear from the initially timid, demure woman.

Following whichever direction she chooses, Asta is led in a circle around the dance floor as Marcy's clumsy steps cause them to wobble out of rhythm with the music. She doesn't seem to notice, and he certainly doesn't care.

It is only as the music slows and the other dancers begin to rock together in a more intimate embrace that Marcy stops her movements.

Keeping his hand firmly anchored on her waist, he asks, "Do we press ourselves together like the others?"

What he would give for the answer to be, 'yes'.

Marcy glances around, grimacing as she focuses on Asta again. "Probably not, since I can't reach your shoulders. But it's okay… because, uh…" she tapers off. Her troubled expression mellows to something more diffident, as though avoiding a question she wishes to ask.

If she is worried that they will be unable to manage the intimate dance together, he can adapt for her. He will ensure she gets to experience everything she wants at this festival, even if he ends up looking like a fool.

In a flash, he scoops her into his arms, bridal-style, and the hem of her dress slips up past her knees. She blushes the deepest shade he has ever seen on her, as her eyes and mouth widen in bewilderment.

"A-Asta!" she gasps, fisting the feathers on his chest to keep her balance.

Summoning a hand through one of his rings, he pulls her hiked dress down past her shins. Although he shouldn't, he allows the pads of his fingers to trace the skin of her calf and ankle on the way down.

Marcy gasps again, but this time, it's stuttered, and she gently pinches her brows together.

"How about this?" he asks, dipping his fox mask closer. "You can reach my neck now, can't you?"

She swallows visibly, with a slight bob in her throat, as her grip on his chest loosens to a relaxed hold.

"Yes, I can reach now," she mutters, leaning against him with her full weight.

He sways their bodies to the music, listening to her deep, trembling breaths, which sometimes whistle as they escape her nose. Her heartbeat thuds against his chest, increasing in tempo as he flexes his fingers against her lower back.

The singer's baritone voice wafts over the crowd like a gentle fog. Marcy hums along while bobbing her feet. It creates a subtle vibration against his skin in a titillating manner, causing him to tighten his grip on her in an unconscious desire to feel more.

He overlooks his possessiveness, relishing in the glow of such a tender connection. And Marcy doesn't seem to mind, either.

When the music stops, Asta almost feels compelled to curse. He wants to touch her more, be *with* her more, but without needing an excuse.

Gently pushing herself away from his chest, Marcy does not ask to be set down. Instead, she averts her eyes as the blush from her cheeks spreads down her neck and up her ears.

"Is there something wrong?" he asks, dragging a knuckle down the column of her neck.

She snorts, seemingly laughing at herself. "Yeah. It's just, um…"

"Tell me what you want, my little lamb," he says, voice honeyed. The hand he used to resituate her skirt remains resting on her ankle, sensually swiping over the bone with his thumb. "I'd be more than happy to oblige any request."

He should not. He knows he should not. But he is helpless when she stares at him with the same prudent look from before. He wants to know what's on her mind, so he can give her everything she desires.

Slapping her hands to her face, Marcy lets out a whining groan. "I don't know if I can. It's embarrassing."

"There is no reason to be discomfit. I cannot feel embarrassment, or at least, not much of it."

Uncertainty hangs in the air, and her fingers part to reveal her worry-filled eyes.

"Say no if it's too much to ask."

"For you? There is no such thing," he replies with a chuckle.

His laughter eases her jittery expression, and she cautiously lowers her hands to her breast.

"I, um…" she starts before taking a deep, steadying breath. "Dancing with you made me more curious about you as a whole, you know?"

He does not follow her meaning but nods as though he does.

"So… what I wanted to ask was…" She clicks her teeth, flashing him an anxious grin. "Can we go somewhere where we can be alone?"

Gods help him.

"The people around us are not real. We are alone now," he replies.

Patting his chest, she stares at his neck like it is the most interesting thing in the world. "I-I know… but it still feels like they're watching us."

He stares at the figures on the dance floor, their blurry faces swaying around them with no discernible features. There is no reason to deny her request, but he suspects she has another motive for wanting to be rid of any prying eyes.

"Do you not wish to dance anymore? I did not think I was *that* terrible," he says, huffing a laugh.

She rolls her bottom lip through her teeth and wraps her arms around his neck again, just like she did during the slow dance. "No, it's not that... When we're pressed together like this, it reminds me how much I enjoy the softness of your feathers."

"You may touch them all you like," he blurts, a little overzealous.

She snickers, tucking her chin. "I've been wanting to ask if I could touch the span of your wings, but I've been too nervous. When I run my hands through your feathers, it makes me wonder what the rest of you feels like, you know?"

Oh, he definitely knows.

"Any human would be curious to know what an 'angel' feels like beneath their fingertips, so there is nothing to be nervous about," he says. The prospect of her hands exploring his body has his every atom shaking.

"It's just that we have a limited time together, and I'd rather spend it learning about one another instead of dancing. Especially since I'm so bad at it," she says, her gaze lifting. "Unless you want to, because another slow dance—"

"I do not care about dancing."

For some reason, she seems surprised by his statement. While she cannot read minds, he thought he was ever so clear about his desire to fulfill her every whim.

"I will take us somewhere private," he says, suppressing the urge to pull her closer. The desire to succumb to lust will not take him, as his need for her favor is much stronger.

"Thank you, Asta. I apologize if my request is a little weird," she says with an impish grimace.

Oh, how he wishes to read her mind, but she did not react well the first time he did.

In truth, if he were to process the full implications of her request, he might vaporize on the spot, just like the bottles he struck in the game. He should expect innocence, even if his restraint is bursting at the seams.

"Of course," he replies, stroking her ankle again. "I will do anything you wish, Marcy."

Chapter 8

Astamesiophelous

Asta has no heart, yet a rapid hammering rattles his rib cage. It is as if there are thousands of birds inside, flapping and thrashing against his torso, trying to escape. The sensation does not diminish as he constructs a private space, utilizing Marcy's memories to create something comfortable, yet entirely new.

The look on her face when the scene is complete is worth the trouble.

Her hands cup her cheeks, her expression filling with amazement. "Asta, this is incredible!" she exclaims, rushing to place her forehead against the glass pane. Staring out the massive window, her smile never falters. "We can see the festival from up here, too!"

Asta joins her at the window, placing his fingertips between her shoulder blades. "You never saw the inside of this building, so I had to improvise."

She rolls her forehead against the window to garner a better look at him, her laughter fogging the glass. "And here I thought we were going back to the blank, white space I arrived in. I never expected you could be this creative."

His chest spasms again, a desire to feel the warmth of her skin suddenly overcoming him.

"As I said before, I want to impress you."

She rolls her eyes, teasingly. "You are full of surprises, aren't you?"

Turning on her heel, Marcy rushes toward the bed that's smothered with lavish, extravagant pillows. She flops on the mound with a bounce, the bed frame squeaking beneath her.

The giggling that pours from her delicate lips could soothe the ocean's most brutal storms. Nothing could compare to the music produced by her happiness, by her affable spirit.

"Come here!" she beckons, snuggling the pillows. "They're so soft, you have to feel them." Her words are muffled by the material after she presses her face into the pile.

The pillows are not what I wish to feel.

Summoning a hand through one of his rings, Asta squeezes the center of a pillow. The texture is neither stimulating nor unpleasant. His unenthused reaction should be expected from one such as himself, a creature formed of feathers.

"They are indeed soft," he states, unable to hide his disinterest. His fascination lies in watching Marcy. She spins and rolls around on top of the bed like an animal in a pile of leaves, swallowed by linen and fluffs of white down.

Asta is quick to notice how the fabric of her dress strains against her thighs and chest. Her movements reveal patches of skin that were once covered. The hem rides up momentarily when she kicks her legs, exposing the waistband of her pale, pink panties. It is not visible for long, but it is enough for him to commit the sight to memory.

A flicker of guilt slows his rings.

Marcy flops onto her back before sitting upright and waving more furiously at him to come join her. "I told you to come here," she says, fussing with the few strands of hair that slipped free. "You said I could feel your wings, remember?"

Creeping closer, the subtle aroma of Marcy's floral perfume frays his nerves. His feathers vibrate and bristle, and the single pillow that now separates them is not enough to quiet his intensifying desire.

I need to calm down.

He tentatively extends his lower wing, the outstretched flight feathers grazing over the comforter next to Marcy.

With both hands hovering a breath away, Marcy looks up at him through her eyelashes. Her mouth curves into a coy smirk as she says, "Your wings are so beautiful, Asta. They remind me of freshly fallen snow."

He has only ever seen snow through the memories of others, including Marcy. He recognizes it as an earthly phenomenon that many humans hold dear, and while he can't understand her fascination with the frozen water, he is more than happy to bask in the glow of the sunny smile the comparison gives her.

Her fingers trace the tops of his wings, and his deep, red eyes give a startled blink. She tilts her head curiously, dragging her touch down the length of his feathers. With her opposite hand, she caresses the bend of his wing, entranced by the subtle white lashes that protect each eye.

It feels like every star concealed beneath his obsidian skin is exploding, going supernova as they attempt to crack and bubble to the surface.

"It has been a very long time since someone touched my feathers willingly," he mumbles.

"Willingly? I never took you as someone to be forceful," she teases as she scoots closer to him. Her legs dangle off the mattress, shoes brushing against his elongated tail feathers.

"Sometimes humans need intervention that requires physical contact," he admits, muscles seizing at her new proximity. He is unable to keep himself calm, but his skittish reactions seem to delight Marcy, so the momentary sting to his pride is a worthy cost.

Her fingers graze the feathers near his neck before fluttering down past his collarbone. He shudders from the simple contact, his torso being the only solid, tactile part of his body, which allows it to feel the most sensations. While his wings have the ability to sense physical touch, it is nothing compared to contact with his chest.

Asta is restless with excitement. The heat from her small hands is warming him to his very core.

She must notice his minute twitches, since she lifts her hands away and timidly asks, "Can I keep going?"

He wishes she would be less hesitant. To stop asking permission and press her body against him already.

"Of course, my little lamb," he says, encircling her with his wings.

At his acquiescence, Marcy flattens her palms against his torso, one hand on either side of the seam in his chest. She raises her brows, and her mouth slips open to form a small "O" as her hands sink into the stark white plumage.

Wiggling her fingers, Asta can't help a huffed laugh in response. He is surprisingly sensitive.

"How does it compare to the pillows?"

Marcy flexes her fingers and slides them over the expanse of his body, her face holding a look of awe. "I never thought I'd be touching an angel. It's like touching beams of sunlight."

She palms and pets his feathers with an innocent eagerness. A gasp occasionally slips from her lips, inquisitive and astounded. Only once she lifts her hands to stroke his neck again does she let out a pleasured moan, mumbling under her breath about the silky texture.

Unbeknownst to her, Asta is drunk with lust. Her touch alone has flustered him, but the sighs she makes are more than enough for him to question how he ever felt ashamed of his growing emotions. Marcy makes him ponder how he could have possibly existed this long without them.

His restraint is rapidly dwindling under the crushing need to touch her. Hands that rarely touch mortal flesh hover over her, begging to fondle her elegant curves. He has no lips or mouth, but he craves to kiss her plump, rose colored lips until she sings his name in ecstasy.

These feelings are...

Scary. Suffocating. *Ravenous.*

Asta flies backward, putting some much-needed space between himself and Marcy.

Even with the full span of the room between them, heat still lingers, begging him to give in to his newfound, primal urges.

Marcy's eyes are wide in stupor while she sits rigid as a statue.

"I'm sorry, did I… do something wrong?" she asks, gradually lowering her hands to her lap.

Pressing his fingers to the spot Marcy was stroking moments prior, he replies, "No, you did nothing wrong. I am not accustomed to being touched. That is all."

That is partially true, but Asta doubts he would have a similar reaction if it were any other human touching him.

"I can relate to that," she says with an empathetic grin. "And I suppose I may have been a little too forceful with you. I apologize."

"You were not forceful," Asta says quickly.

Setting aside his nauseating anxiety, he inches back toward Marcy. If she knew half of the inappropriate thoughts he was conjuring about her, she might not be so kind.

Marcy crosses one leg over the other and does not readjust her dress to cover her now-exposed knees. She bobs her foot, drawing circles with the toe of her shoe.

"You know, you can touch me, too, if that'll make you feel less self-conscious. I know you're curious," she says, darting her gaze to the floor as her cheeks flush bright red. The blush quickly travels down her neck and chest until it reaches the tops of her breasts, which are almost heaving from her heavy breaths.

Asta nearly plummets to the ground at her offer, unable to stop himself from hovering closer to her once more.

"I do not share the same curiosity for your anatomy as you have for mine," he murmurs.

She closes her eyes and allows her head to loll to the side, pressing her cheek into her shoulder with a laugh. "That's not what I meant, Asta."

Tilting his rings in inquiry, his entire being melts to liquid once she looks up at him, a demure sparkle in her dark pupils.

She offers him her hand. Her voice is soft and seductive as she says, "I want you to touch me, Asta. For pleasure."

Chapter 9

Marcy

She nervously twists her necklace around her index finger, biting down on the inside of her cheek. She has never been the one to initiate intimacy, but her ardent request came with a new, unexpected confidence. She feels assured in her forwardness though, given how much Asta has been spoiling her.

A euphoric look explodes across the eyes on Asta's wings. They blink rapidly in disbelief as his pupils grow to become the size of dinner plates.

While she knows he no longer misunderstands her, that doesn't help with her own unease. Nor the tingling sensation that is rapidly spreading through her fingertips.

Marcy fights against the words of denial that are attempting to bubble up her throat. The urge to ignore her desires, to ensure she won't face rejection, sears her like a red-hot brand.

"I'd like to be intimate with you, Asta," she forces herself to say, even if she cannot meet his stare. "Before this is all over. Before I'll never see you again."

She nearly jumps out of her skin when a hand rests upon her hip, her gaze snapping to the point of contact.

"Requesting intimacy with an ethereal being — or an 'angel', as you call it?" His low chuckle is smooth with amusement. "You never cease to surprise me, my little lamb. But you do not know what you ask."

Someone may as well light Marcy on fire. Being scorched by a pillar of flames would surely be cooler than the current level of heat prickling her skin, threatening to incinerate her.

She cannot even *begin* to imagine what a sexual experience with an angel would entail, let alone *this* angel. Granted he agrees to her request.

"I know what I'm asking for," she says, teeth sinking into her lower lip. "For as long as I've lived, I never wanted anyone the way I want you."

This is so embarrassing, she thinks, her chest tight.

Asta says nothing, but his hand gives her hip a gentle squeeze, urging her to continue.

"You may not be a human, or even a man, but I can't deny my feelings." Marcy dares to look up at him, momentarily startled by the blinding glow of his red eyes. "In the short time we've spent together, I've experienced more joy than every feeble, pathetic moment of my life, *combined*. I never thought I'd be able to laugh so much, to smile until my cheeks hurt, or to care so much that someone might enjoy my baking." She pauses to weave her fingers through Asta's. "I never thought I'd want to be touched by someone ever again."

While not explicitly stated, there is a plea to her words, a deep longing voiced with such passion that she barely recognizes herself.

"If you're going to deny me, my only request is that you be kind," she mumbles, sinking into herself.

Placing a finger beneath her chin, Asta lifts her gaze to meet the stare of his bull mask. The horns cast a shadow over her face as he extends his wingspan to its full length, his sheer size dwarfing her small frame.

"I could never deny you, Marcy. Surely, you have realized that by now," he says in a rumbling, throaty voice. Using his thumb and forefinger to turn her head, he presses the bull's snout against her ear. "I would like nothing more than to please you."

Goosebumps crawl over her skin, and a shiver runs down her spine.

"You make it sound like a duty," she says, puffing her cheeks. "I only want to if *you* want to. Not because you are forced to comply with my demands."

Another of his massive hands trails down her chest, while the one holding her chin moves over her jaw, wrapping around her face. Drawing back so that she can see both his masks, his voice is authoritative as he states, "I am not human. I have only ever been a witness to humanity and their experiences. My kind would view the lust I feel as shameful and would call for my immediate reconstruction." He brushes his thumb over her cheek before he continues. "But there are no words in any language, human or ethereal, that can describe the horrors I would face if it meant I could experience these emotions again with you. Believe me when I say that this is not duty. This is desire."

She pouts, the corners of her lips quivering. "Asta..."

"I am too human for my own good. My emotions may eventually come to devastate me or lead to my destruction. I cannot guarantee the future or that I will do anything correctly. I will need to rely on you for guidance, but I am eager to learn... if my inexperience is something you can accept." He speaks with an air of innocence, like how a virgin would speak to their first partner.

I suppose he is a virgin.

Marcy can't help the giddy smile that comes to her face at the prospect of being his first. Something about his thinly veiled nervousness, which he tries to mask behind stoic conviction, makes her heart soar. She knows how badly he wants her approval, for her to look at him with fondness.

If only he knew how much I desire him too.

Flicking the nose ring of his bull mask, she hooks her finger through the metal to pull it closer. "I have to ask..." Her thumb strokes the cutouts of the bull's nose as she clicks her tongue. "Do you have...?"

"A penis? No."

She must appear disappointed when she replies with a soft, "Oh," because he is frantic to clarify his statement.

"I have erogenous zones. The gods are not cruel enough to deny us the opportunity for carnal pleasure, but it is not anatomy you are used to," he explains.

Marcy presses a delicate kiss to the bull mask's snout, before resting her forehead against it.

Asta's groan is akin to a gasp, uttered in a way that someone might react as if kissed by a life-long crush. There is such sweetness in his hushed pants and the way his rings spin out of control with excitement.

"Can you show me?" she asks, pressing another kiss to the bull's cheek. "I can make you feel good, too."

Her back hits the pillows, and Asta places his palm firmly on her abdomen. A grunt is forced from her mouth, her cheeks reddening even more, if possible.

"A-Asta!" she exclaims with a playful laugh, wetting her lips as he looms over her.

Creating hands in an array of sizes, and enough to fill each of his extra rings, he places them all around her. Mischief flashes in his many eyes, but the distinct gravel of lust drips from his voice.

"My own satisfaction is of little interest to me," he grunts, trailing a finger down her neck. "Your pleasure is what I want. Your moans, pants, cries, anything and everything you are willing to give me until there is nothing left. To see you overcome with euphoria, drowning in bliss while begging for more." One of his many hands pauses at the collar of her dress, its three small buttons obstructing his path. "*That* is how you can make me feel good, Marcy."

She swallows hard, her lips parting. "Oh my," she squeaks.

The hand attached to his torso flashes its palm, the swarm of stars within his skin coalescing there. Deep in concentration, he forces the stars to flicker and swirl into a foreign shape. The light parts, revealing a slit within the palm, and what looks to be a tongue. The appendage is a striking blue, vibrant against the obsidian of his palms.

He does the same with another hand, the tongues lazily rolling out from between the slit-like lips. The sight sends a bolt of electricity straight to her core. She teems with anticipation.

"I'm not the greatest at matter manipulation, but these are adequate, no?" he asks, applying a mouthed palm to the supple skin of her neck.

The lips contort around her throat with a sloppy wetness, but he is careful not to press against her too roughly. His tongue swipes along the length of her neck, providing the same tingling sensation she feels when touching his skin.

Her lips part with a moan, eyelids slamming shut as her back arches against the pillows. She shudders, her lower body throbbing with need. Need for more.

"Tell me how to please you, Marcy," Asta purrs, allowing his tongue to ravage the taut lines of her throat. Multiple hands hover over her, awaiting her instruction. "Where do you like to be touched?"

The question causes her to snap open her eyes, and she presses her lips together in an awkward smile. "I, um, don't know, to be honest. I've never had a man touch me in a way I liked. Or even try to do anything I might like, for that matter," she admits.

"Have you ever reached climax?" he asks, his tone as blasé as someone asking about the weather.

How like him to speak so bluntly, she thinks, pinching her lips to suppress a smile.

"No, Asta. Never," she replies.

His fingers fidget, and Marcy notes the complete elation in his voice when he says, "Then I am overjoyed to be the first to give you that experience."

Her heart soars with excitement at the sound of his completely unfounded confidence. No matter how antsy he may be, he doesn't move an inch without her expressed permission.

Marcy peels the hand from her neck, allowing it to float back to the others, then sits upright on the bed. Leaning forward, she unbuttons her heels, making sure to give him an eyeful of her cleavage. She drags her hands up her legs, kicking her shoes off to the side.

The hunger in his gaze makes her feel like the sexiest woman who's ever lived. She is loving every moment of this.

Slipping a finger under her collar, she pops the first button of her dress. Asta stiffens, his rings twirling as he watches her. She unties the built-in fabric belt at her waist, then plucks open the second and third buttons. Pressing her thighs together, she tries, and fails, to quell the heat pooling at her center. She never had a reason to feel like the simple act of undressing could be seductive until now.

Pushing at his chest, she urges Asta to allow her the room to stand. He doesn't understand her intention but obliges her request.

The lump in her throat tightens as she rises, and anticipation causes a trembling in her knees. She unhooks the final ties of her dress, the fabric falling to hang loosely against her chest.

Dropping her dress, the material pools at her ankles. Only her pink panties and matching bra are left to cover her body.

Marcy stands tall, nearly bare, before Asta. She feels hot all over, her skin desperate for the touch of his tongue. While she's too afraid to ask him directly, she knows he wants the same thing, since the stars of his skin are glowing as bright as his eyes.

He does not move an inch. Does not say a word.

"You're making me nervous," she laughs. "Do you, um, like it?"

Asta's fingers flex wildly, knuckles practically bursting from his skin. "I do. Very much."

"Then why aren't you doing anything?" she asks awkwardly.

Chest heaving, he replies, "Because I will not do anything without your command."

Marcy presses her palms to her cheeks, skin smoldering. She forgot how many times he told her that all he wants is *her* approval — her only experience with men being those who *take* what they want.

The way Asta treats her, so gentle and eager, will be her undoing. If she were a more self-assured woman, she'd jump him here and now.

She presses her lips together as she sits back down on the bed. Leaning back, she props herself up on her elbows and lowers her gaze.

Her confidence surging with the allure of his attention, she whispers, "Asta, can you help me feel good?"

Chapter 10

Astamesiophelous

He nearly cries out with relief at her sultry demand.

The immense internal pressure of his impatience has him nearly disintegrating into stardust. It would be a painful death, but it would be a more than satisfying way to die. Simply watching Marcy strip already has him much too close to combustion.

Extending both of the arms attached to his torso, Asta's fingers hover over her rib cage.

"I am unsure of what you like. Please place my hands on the areas that will bring you the most enjoyment," he says. His hands tremble as her chest rises and falls with her panting, her searing-hot flesh inching closer to his touch.

Her cheeks pinch, and the slight upturn of her lips grows in size when she tugs one of his hands to the thin fabric covering her breasts. "Like I said before, no man's touch has ever been enjoyable for me, so I can't really answer that." A devilish look fills her eyes when she repeats her earlier question, "Can you help me find what feels good?"

Asta has never had such an immediate answer to a question before. The answer is yes. It is always yes, for her. But he must not lose his composure. He is no beast.

"I would love to," he says, his eagerness causing his voice to lift to a higher pitch. "But if something feels bad, will you let me know?"

Marcy nibbles her lower lip before whisking away the indentation she created with a swipe of her tongue. How he wishes he had infinite mouths to taste the trail of saliva she left behind.

"Of course I will. You have my full trust, Asta." Her eyelashes flutter. Her face glows like a beacon, begging to be kissed.

I am no better than a perverted human male, he thinks, enthralled by her beauty.

Large, careful hands slide across the expanse of her bra, the lace soft against his skin. Following the elastic band to her back, he unhooks the clasps, resisting the urge to rip the fabric in two. He longs to bask in the sight of her, to worship her in a way that would put her god to shame. But he must not be hasty. He needs to savor this. Savor *her.*

Marcy gasps when the material comes undone, her chest reddening in a blush.

"I didn't think you'd know how to do that."

"I know many things," he says cheekily, elated that she is impressed. He may or may not have just been lucky, having never seen such a device before. But he'll never tell.

Marcy shrugs her shoulders, the straps of her bra slinking down her arms until the obstructing fabric falls to the side. Bashful, a blush rises to her ears, coating her pale olive complexion with warm undertones.

For the first time since meeting her, Asta is glad that he is immortal. If he were flesh and blood, he does not doubt that such a gorgeous sight would stop his beating heart. He can't help but stare, unconcerned by how strange his gawking might look.

Her breasts are petite and teardrop-shaped, perfectly suited to her long torso and pronounced collarbone. Just above her chest, lines of lighter skin highlight where she's bathed in the sun, with subtle freckles peppering her shoulders. Trailing his fingers down her stomach, he notices purplish stripes of skin that wrap around her waist and slither up her hips. Each wrinkle and mark describes the complexity of her life better than any memory ever could. If he had infinite time, he'd learn every detail, trace every path with his tongue until it was second nature.

He is grateful that Marcy is his last evaluation. Otherwise, he would spend the rest of his existence carving her body and soul into everything he touched. Even when he is inevitably turned into stardust, he is not entirely sure he will not search for pieces of her amongst the stars.

Steadily, while gauging her expression, Asta places a mouthed hand against the underside of her breast, weighing it in his palm. A breathy gasp hitches her chest, and goosebumps break out over her flesh. Running his fingertips over the raised bumps, his feathers ruffle.

The mouth he formed on one of his hands sucks the delicate skin while the other playfully trails its tongue along her other breast. Intrigued by her little spasms, he thumbs over her nipples. The swelling buds are a deep shade of mauve, and they turn even more red as he flicks and pinches them with interest. The surrounding skin is soft, like the petals of a flower, encircled with minuscule bumps.

"A-ah!" she flinches, her fingers clenching the bedspread.

Marcy's eyes flutter shut, her thighs pressing together with each lap of his tongue. Only when one of his mouths grazes over her erect nipple does she sigh a moan, stifling the noise by biting her knuckle as her cheeks flush deeper.

Seeing her enjoyment, Asta takes the peak of her other nipple between his fervid lips. He rolls the buds between his teeth, entranced by the way her shoulders loll and her back arches for more.

All the while, her lip remains pressed between her teeth in restraint.

With a free hand, he tugs on Marcy's lower lip with his thumb, freeing it from the pressure.

Eyes flicking open, her brows lift.

He swipes over her wet, swollen lip, chucking her chin and forcing her gaze to his. "There's no need to hide your voice," he says, drifting his touch down her collarbone to her abdomen. "I quite like the sounds you make and would be delighted to hear more."

Marcy's eyes widen. "It's embarrassing. The noises, I mean," she whispers.

Halting above her panty line, his masks and main ring dip to the side. "Is it? One does not strum an instrument unless they intend to make it sing."

Bursting into laughter, Marcy's chest shakes beneath his grasp. The hesitation that froze her muscles melts away, and her lips form a sweet smile.

"Did I... say something funny?"

Although confused, he's grateful he made her happy.

She shakes her head, falling to her elbows after she pulls the last pins from her hair, allowing it to fall freely. The honey-brown strands tumble past her shoulders before she whisks them away. "I've never met a man like you," she says.

"I am not a man," he deadpans.

"Of course not, Asta," Marcy says seductively. Gaze half-lidded, amusement twitches her lips.

He doesn't need to be a man to see that she wants him to continue, her hips rotating in small circles beneath the press of his fingertips. If she wants more, he will gladly oblige, and he hopes to be bathed in her vocal encouragements.

Stilled palms taunt her with a flick of his tongue, sucking and teasing until she finally lets out an uninhibited moan.

A bolt of lightning sizzles down Asta's spine, causing a tingling sensation to pool within him. He is already addicted to her cries of pleasure, and his hands move on their own to discover what other reactions he can extract from her body.

Hooking his fingers through the waistband of her panties, he tugs the silken fabric down her legs. He tosses the garment over his shoulder, not caring where it lands.

Marcy gasps, snapping her thighs together as she moves to cover herself with her hands.

"There's no need to be nervous. I will go slow," Asta coaxes, running his middle finger up the seam of her thighs. "Trust me, my little lamb."

She takes a heaving breath. The strained muscles of her face soften until the wrinkles smooth. Her response is a subtle nod and a hum; her voice lost to her anxiety. Urging him to carry on, she parts her legs without a word.

Gods, he is close to coming undone.

Grasping her ankles, he rests her feet on either side of his neck. He palms her thighs, softly stroking the supple skin. Pressing down until her skin gives way, he trails his touch higher, until he's a hairsbreadth from her entrance.

She freezes, expression unreadable. It is almost as if her mind is somewhere else entirely.

"Are you alright?" he prods.

Her nod is stilted, but she looks upset.

"Marcy, look at me," he says with a gentle command. She does, and the hollow abyss of her pupils exposes the depth of her anxiety.

She shivers, and the color drains from her face. "I'm sorry, I don't know why I'm like this," she says, her voice wobbling.

"Why are you apologizing?" he asks with a wince. "There is no need to be sorry. We can stop and even return to the festival, if you would like. All I want is to spend time with you."

Seeing Marcy so tense pains him. He does not need to know why, only how to guide her out of the shell she created for herself. She's not alone anymore, and he wants to prove it to her.

"You'd be okay with that?" she whispers, her brows pinched. Despite her tight expression, the stony ice in her gaze slowly melts.

His eyes squint at her in puzzlement, his tone not hiding his confusion. "Of course. Am I not supposed to be okay with that?"

With those simple words, life returns to her eyes. The dull, vacant look now blossoms into a brilliant shine, highlighting the smoky quartz color of her irises. She laughs with a snort, scrubbing her face with the heel of her palms.

She begins to apologize again but stops herself. "We don't need to stop, Asta," she says, pressing a kiss to his hand. "I'm okay now. I just needed a moment, I think."

Relief softens the tension inside him, grateful she is no longer wearing the same forlorn look as when she first arrived for her evaluation. He enjoys her confident side, unafraid to tell him what she wants, and uninhibited by fear.

"I promise I'll be gentle. Whatever you need," he reassures her with a soft squeeze.

Her eyes glimmer with tears, but she's quick to blink them away. "Thank you," she says warmly. "You can continue."

While he's always made sure to pay special attention to the nuances of her facial expressions, he understands that now it is more pertinent than ever. Her confidence may have grown, but that's no reason for him to overlook the subtle ways she expresses her discomfort and fears.

"I said you can continue," she mumbles with her chin tucked against her chest, blushing fiercely.

He cannot help but chuckle, elated to hear the slight demand in her voice.

"No need to be impatient," he teases.

She shoots him a nonplussed look, followed by a giggle. He's new to teasing, but she seems to have enjoyed it.

Asta slowly resumes the tentative pace of his descent to her lower abdomen, fondling her breasts with a gentle wave of his fingers. She releases a slow, steadying breath until she melts back into the comforter.

"Very good, Marcy," he praises, noting how relaxed she appears.

In a single swipe, he grazes her clit with a feather-light touch. The sudden pressure makes her flinch, but she mewls enthusiastically despite her modest smile.

He wants to see more of her expressions. No, *needs* to.

Becoming bolder, he slides a finger through her folds, savoring the wet warmth he finds there. Marcy is boiling to the touch, her slick arousal coating the inside of her thighs.

He ventures to slip inside, pushing his middle finger past the seam of her entrance, up to his first knuckle.

She inhales sharply, then slaps her hands atop his, forcing him to squeeze her breasts harder. She increases the pressure until he finally acquiesces to her silent begging.

"Asta," she breathes, chewing the inside of her cheek.

His name from her mouth shoots a bolt of desire through every nerve in his wings. The faint glow of his eyes intensifies, painting her with a dull light.

"Please, keep saying my name," he whispers.

"*Asta.*"

The sound kisses his skin, the melody carrying the wanting words her mouth refuses to speak. He sinks his finger deeper, needing to draw out more of her lovely sounds. When his knuckle brushes her pelvis, he curls his fingertip, then flexes it straight again.

Marcy groans louder, more guttural, then turns her head into the pile of pillows behind her. Her legs squirm as he continues to stroke her, trapping her ankles on his shoulders with another pair of hands. At this point, he's lost track of how many hands he has summoned. There will never be enough, even if his hands cover every inch of her body.

Slowly adding his ring finger, he uses both digits to work her with salacious, torturous intent. Her hips buck at the additional pressure, her body easily giving in to his intrusion. He is soon able to pump his fingers into her without an ounce of resistance.

Her insides are silken, quivering. Her brow furrows, and her pants grow frantic. He curls his fingers again, and as her pussy bears down on him, a sensual whimper escapes from her lips.

"Marcy," he murmurs, barely audible. "Can I make you come?"

Her eyes flutter open, revealing the shine of a single tear in the corner of her eye. "If you can," she replies with a doubtful grimace.

Asta's knowledge of human anatomy may be limited, but he has witnessed more than his fair share of sexual encounters through his evaluations. And now that he has a taste for what Marcy enjoys, seeing her fall apart from pleasure is his only goal.

He presses a kiss to her cheek with a mouthed palm, readying another above her pussy.

"Quite bold of you to doubt the capabilities of an ethereal being, especially considering your current position," he chuckles, nodding at the visible wet spot that has formed on the sheets between her thighs.

His rings twirl faster when she smirks at his quip.

"Okay, Asta. Prove me wrong," she taunts, her tongue sliding over her top lip.

Gods. I love it when she feels confident.

Determination licks his skin with heated flames.

He started slowly to make Marcy comfortable, but now he increases his pace with a steady focus. His knuckles press against her pelvis, rocking her back and forth with the aid of the bedsprings. Her breasts bounce beneath the expanse of his palms, which begin to fondle her more roughly to match the speed at which he fingers her.

Marcy throws back her head, a throaty grunt ripping from her chest. "*Oh my god,*" she chokes out, rolling her hips against his hands.

Her nails bite into his arm when he grazes a sensitive spot inside her, muscles convulsing and fighting against his firm hold. She wets her lips, and her whiny moans fill the room, joining the wet sound of his fingers pumping inside her as she meets him thrust for thrust. If he were to stop all movement, he is sure she would gladly pleasure herself against his fingers all on her own.

"God, Asta," she groans, her eyes rolling into the back of her head.

An additional hand dips between her legs, the mouth on its palm stretched wide with a protruding tongue, ready to taste her. His lips latch onto her swollen clit, suckling at the sensitive nub.

Her reaction is immediate, grinding against him feverishly until the covers beneath her spread into a disheveled circle. He continues to suck on her bundle of nerves, pairing it with an increase in pressure from the mouths nibbling her nipples.

When her moans become more guttural, he is certain that she is enjoying his subdued brutishness. No longer trying to hide herself, she puts her trust in him, completely. And he will prove himself worthy of her trust, if only so they can do this again.

Happily taking whatever he gives her, Asta finds and teases every spot that makes her chest quiver and legs spasm. His hands cover every inch of her skin, licking, squeezing, and caressing the dips and swells of her flesh, etching the shapes into his memory.

"You are so beautiful," he murmurs as his palm starts to vibrate against her clit.

Marcy's moans turn into sobs before she clamps her thighs around his hand. Her eyelids lift shakily to meet his oppressive gaze.

The lust in those sepia-brown eyes could melt him, leaving nothing but a puddle on the floor. The words spilling from her lips are unintelligible, every bit incoherent and overpowered by complete bliss.

Asta stiffens his wrist, preparing to bring her to climax. If the expression on her face when she comes is half as alluring as the look she's giving him now, a single orgasm will not be enough to satisfy his desire.

Teeth pinch her nipples, causing red marks to blossom around each breast. The hue deepens with the forceful way his mouths start sucking on her skin, leaving even more distinct marks in their wake. Simultaneously, his tongue soothes the throbbing ache of her clit, delicately lapping at the quivering nub as his fingers ravage her.

"Asta, I think I'm going to—" Cut off by an empty scream, Marcy's mouth forms an "O". Her body shudders, toes curling and throat flexing.

She is almost over the edge, but not quite.

"Get there for me, my little lamb," he coaxes, stroking her thighs to ease the tension in her.

The whisper of tears grows to a swell, and she pinches her brows and forehead as she ruts against his hands like an animal in heat. She has lost any bashfulness she had about the noises she is making, screaming and groaning as she chases her release.

One calculated swipe over the clustered nerves inside her is all it takes for Marcy to unravel before his very eyes.

"Oh god! Oh god!" she screams until her voice dies out. Her core clenches tightly around his fingers, nearly snapping them clean off. Her soft, tender flesh convulses around him in a broken rhythm. Clawing at the sheets, she arches onto her shoulders and thrusts her hips as she gasps for air.

As he expected, she looks extraordinary during climax. Her chin is lifted, neck craning against the mattress, her tongue pressed to her palate. Her messy hair lies strewn about, the strands pooling around her clenched jaw, gracefully framing her erotic expression.

He stares, drinking in the sight of her, and gods, he can't get enough.

Asta works her through her orgasm, massaging the same spot that had just given her release. The vein on her neck thrums with her rapidly beating heart, and she moans softly as he drags out her pleasure. Her muscles finally settle, the aftershocks a feeble shake in comparison.

Only once she is satisfied does she sink into the mattress, sweat beading along her cheeks and forehead. Tear stains streak down her temples, and her face is flushed and glowing.

He pops his mouths off her breasts, drinking in the swollen, budding peaks that glisten and drip with his saliva. Little red marks dot her skin, mostly from mouths that got a little too carried away.

The sight of his marks on her skin arouses him, and his hands flex with the compulsion to bring her to euphoria again.

Marcy lazily drapes her arms over her chest, not intending to cover herself, but rather to self-soothe. She breathes heavily, and the rise and fall of her chest becomes more subtle as time passes.

"That was incredible," she says with a giggle, wiping away the dribbles of sweat from her brow.

"I am pleased to know that," he says, attempting to play coy by hiding his jubilation. "You know I want to impress you."

Marcy lays sprawled across the bed, sighing in contentment. "You always seem to."

Asta's ego inflates far beyond the acceptable size for an ethereal being.

"I never knew sex could be like that," she continues, her face pinching ever so slightly with the pang of embarrassment. "Since you're the first to make me…" she rotates her wrist in a circle, motioning her hand, *"you know."*

He winces. "How the universe can be so cruel to such a pretty thing is astonishing," he says, stroking the length of her calf. "We must make up for lost time then, no?"

Marcy sucks her lips into her mouth, snorting in amused surprise. "You've become so bold, Asta." She smirks. "But what else can we do? You don't have a penis."

Her excitement to explore more sexual experiences with him makes his rings spin, and he hastily replies, "I may not have genitals, but I have something you may enjoy much more."

Chapter 11

Marcy

She watches Asta with lips parted in anticipation. The fingers that were inside of her moments ago plunge into his palm, his mouth gaping with excitement. His bluish tongue swirls and laps at the digits feverishly, sucking them until he's collected every last drop. Heat flares in his eyes as he savors her taste, and a possessive grip clutches her waist.

She can't help but stare. His wings shiver as though he's devouring a decadent sweet, humming softly through his full mouth. The wildfire raging inside her grows in ferocity. His inability to hide his enthusiasm and desire for her is astonishingly sexy.

Once his fingers are licked clean, he positions a wide ring between them. With a crackle, two hands push from the center of the hollow ring, palms facing forward.

"Are your hands sensitive?" she inquires, hesitant to touch the star-speckled skin. She allows her fingers to graze the new appendages, and he shudders.

"My normal hands are as sensitive as a human's. This pair, however, is different."

He extends the arms at his torso in comparison, and Marcy understands what he means. The hands protruding from this ring are thinner than the others, fingers elongated and rounded with little curvature.

She tilts her head. "Is this what you meant by an 'erogenous zone'?"

Wiggling the rounded fingers, he nods. "I am able to concentrate many nerves into one central point, creating something much like human genitals."

A blush prickles her cheeks at the thought of touching him the same way he pleasured her. Her heart races, eager to make him feel just as good.

"Why are there two?" she asks, drawing back to take him in. "Surely that will be a difficult fit."

A deep chuckle rumbles from Asta's chest, and the sound sends desire flooding down her spine to the warmth between her thighs. The melody of his laughter draws such a carnal craving from her. She'd be mortified if he didn't just see her orgasm for the first time.

"I still have to *make* my genitals," he says with a smile in his voice. "Watch carefully."

Sitting upright, Marcy tucks her feet beneath her. She leans forward in excitement, and a small twinge of fear, at what's to come. The thought of seeing what he will create, an erotic piece of him, turns her on.

His dark hands press their palms together as if in prayer, melding until there is no space left between them. The two wrists twist in opposite directions, fingers wrapping around the backside of his palms until they grasp one another in a firm hold.

The dark hue of his deep, galaxy-like skin begins to glow, and a vibrant blue color crawls up the base, devouring each fingertip. Only once the stars reappear against his vivid blue skin do the fingers begin to stretch, wrapping around the base in a subtle spiral.

The fingers shift, morphing into deep grooves, like vines twisting together on an old tree. Little rounded offshoots protrude in all directions, twitching as the entire length bobs up and down while being kept stable by a thick knot at the base.

The final transformation is breathtaking and completely inhuman. Marcy's tongue darts between her lips. She wonders what he will taste like. Will he be gentle and let her set the pace? Or will he roughly thrust himself down her throat? She balls her hands together in restraint, until her knuckles go white.

Mustering the courage to speak, her voice barely breaks the surrounding silence when she utters, "It's striking."

His eyes widen in worry before narrowing slightly. "Is that a good thing…?" he asks gingerly, sounding exposed, vulnerable.

It is more than *good* — it is quite possibly the most visually stunning appendage she's ever seen. If the version of herself that existed in her mortal life knew that she would be in awe of an angel's penis, she'd have perished on the spot.

"It's a wonderful thing, Asta," Marcy clarifies, stroking the underside of his cock with a light touch.

The texture feels like gelatin, but a bit firmer. And while he is warm, it is not hotter than the temperature of her palm. She traces the span of his length before flicking the converging tip. A satisfied smile curves her lips.

"Where do you like to be touched—" Her words are cut off by Asta's gruff groan.

Her name floats through the air in a melody, but a series of gasps and grunts quickly obscure it. His hands flex, then go rigid, as though willing himself into control by ripping at the air.

The tendrils extending from his base begin to wiggle, building in alacrity until they are nearly vibrating. His wings lengthen and his torso straightens, every inch of him locking up as he tries to swallow the noises he is making.

His chest and wings tremble before his cock jerks, straining, and a stream of hot, viscous liquid bursts from his tip. The release coats Marcy's chin and breasts. The fluid brings cool relief to her burning skin.

Looking down, her eyes go wide as she stares at the glowing liquid with awe. A familiar blue color paints her in neon tones, as if the stars that make up his being suddenly surged out of his cock. She then notices that while he is still erect, his lighter colors do not shine as brightly as they did moments ago.

"*Ah, Marcy,*" he moans as the tight swell at the base of his cock pulsates like a heartbeat.

Asta's muscles relax, but his dick remains hard and throbbing, clearly unsatisfied. His chest puffs out, and with an aura of mortification, he averts his many eyes.

Marcy touches the liquid dribbling from her chin in fascination, before bringing a few drops to her tongue. It's tasteless, but in the same way someone might describe water: light and clean. She assesses Asta, who seems to have overcome his embarrassment enough to intensely observe her while she rolls his release over her tongue.

"I am so sorry. T-that doesn't normally happen to me," he frets with cum still dripping from his tip.

Marcy lifts her brows as a dark cloud of jealousy explodes in her chest. "*Normally?* I thought you said you've never done this with anyone before?" she demands. She's aware that her tone is accusatory, but she doesn't care.

There is no time for her fears to develop or fester, as Asta dissolves them with a single shake of his masks. "Not with *anyone,* no. But I have indulged in auto-erotic pleasure." He tucks his wings timidly. "Which is something I find myself doing often as of late. Further evidence that I am becoming more human."

She never expected to feel so relieved by his answer, but she is even more relieved that he appears to be experiencing the same nervous arousal that she is.

I sound like a teenager with a crush, she thinks, despite her goofy smile.

Being inexperienced can be foreboding, especially when it involves sex, but with Asta, she's more than excited to explore the very things she was once repulsed by.

Taking one of his hands in both of hers, she strokes it comfortingly. "If you can keep going, there is a lot more for us to enjoy," she says, bowing her head over the tip of his cock. She presses a soft kiss to the top, the blue flesh still sticky.

Asta forces her head back, forming a taut string of his release between her mouth and his dick. He doesn't do it out of surprise, but rather, in discouragement.

"No," he starts, running his fingers over her scalp then through the ends of her hair. "This is about *you*. My satisfaction is irrelevant."

"Well, that doesn't seem fair, does it?" she questions, nudging her cheek into one of his palms. "I want to return the favor."

Taking her face between his thumb and index finger, he tilts her head. Swiping his thumb over her jawline, he savors the feel of her skin.

"If you wish to reciprocate, then by all means, but use me for *your* pleasure." A hint of need flashes in his eyes. His voice becomes husky, almost on the edge of a whine, as he says, "*I beg of you.*"

All she can do is nod. Coherent thoughts melt into a single, fervorous need for her to take him, to enjoy him in the way they both burn for. If he is willing to beg her to use him for her own pleasure, who is she to deny him? He is responsible for her current lustfulness, eliciting a drive she thought dead and buried long ago.

The flame Asta set ablaze within her roars with an intensity she can't extinguish. And God, she doesn't want to.

Chapter 12

Marcy

Lifting herself into a kneeling position, she grabs either side of the ring encircling his cock and pulls it toward her. She presses the backside into the covers, giving him a steady place to balance. His length brushes her stomach when she readjusts, causing a bead of her arousal to slide down the inside of her thigh.

She never thought she would get so hot and bothered while taking control, but teasing Asta to the point of shuddering and whimpering before he even enters her makes the pleasure she's about to feel that much richer.

Hissing with a tight jaw, Marcy continues to raise her hips until he is positioned directly beneath her. With half-lidded eyes, she stares up at him as she orients his cock with a gentle nudge.

His tip bumps against her wetness, and he releases a gasp that makes it sound like he is on the verge of tears.

"Can I...?" she trails off, dipping her head to the side.

"You are in control. Do as you please," he says, voice trembling as he cradles her hips, squeezing the supple skin.

His poor attempt at hiding his nerves is charming and helps ease the fluttering butterflies that are tormenting her insides.

Dropping her hips, the tip of his cock spears her opening. His flailing tendrils lick her gluttonously, trying desperately to pull her further down his shaft. She throws her head back with a breathy moan when a single tendril strays from the base, grazing her clit.

Asta takes her breasts in his palms, thumbing over her pebbled nipples the way he knows she likes. "Lovely, my little lamb. Take as long as you need to adjust," he coos.

At first glance, Marcy didn't think his size was too abnormal. But now that he is stretching her to capacity, she realizes just how enormous he is. Her only saving grace is his pliability, the girth molding to fill any open space. And this is still just the tip.

"Relax."

Raising her head, Marcy meets his patient, adoring stare. He looks at her as though she, herself, created the universe. His eyes hold an overwhelming amount of affection.

He tenderly strokes her hips and thighs, attempting to coax her into a more comfortable position. It's like he's afraid to break her, treating her as if she were a porcelain figurine. She can't help but chortle at his concern as she leisurely yanks a spare hand by the wrist to meet her cheek.

If he won't be brave, then she will.

"Can you make a mouth on this palm?"

His wings stutter, but his response is immediate. "For you, always."

Like a parting sea, the rich, light-speckled skin slithers open, and a wide tongue emerges through the slit, curling at the tip.

Marcy smiles mischievously, her eyes darting between Asta and the newly formed mouth. Tightening her grip on his wrist, she holds it in place so he can't pull away.

Focusing on the subtle flickering of light in his eyes, she further impales herself on his cock, gliding down until he's halfway inside her. She takes him easily, his flesh expanding to fill every inch as her lower abdomen domes from the size.

He feels *amazing*. Her mind is blank, endorphins heightening all her senses at once.

God. He hasn't even started moving yet.

Her disheveled grin turns slack when the thrashing tendrils protruding from his cock massage her most sensitive spots. They diligently work to open her, pushing at her walls until she effortlessly falls onto the top of his knotted base. Her thighs slap against his ring, and her arousal coats his bulging knot as she squeezes around him. Hard.

"Oh my God, Asta," she moans, goosebumps breaking out over her entire body. She rocks against him, the slight movement sending shockwaves through her and weakening her knees.

Feathers glide across her breasts, teasing them until the pebbles of her skin grow more pronounced. He traces her cheekbone with his knuckle, wiping away an escaped tear.

"Breathtaking," he murmurs, admiring her facial features with his touch, as though she were a sculpture.

She glances down at where they are connected, and that is all it takes for her last thread of composure to snap. The daunting, bright blue flesh that seemed much too large has disappeared inside her, and his knot twitches as tendrils at the base vie for entry.

His wiggling bulge presses visibly beneath the skin of her stomach, creating a delicious, consuming fullness that makes her mouth water. In every sense, she is bursting at the seams.

Climax builds prematurely at the base of her spine, her thighs tense and expectant. But she doesn't want to finish alone.

Wrapping her hand behind Asta's neck, she tugs him closer until his silken feathers collide with her chest. His masks spin with curiosity as she presses his mouthed hand to her lips.

He cries out softly, tongue frozen against his palate.

"I-I don't know how—" he starts, cut off by Marcy brushing her tongue against the tip of his.

She molds her mouth against his, holding up her index finger to halt his objections. He's clearly nervous, denoted by his tottering rings and constantly wandering eyes. It's adorable.

But as much as he may want to impress her, it's time for her to take the lead.

After a few more shy attempts at resisting her control, Asta finally concedes.

"If it's unpleasant, I apologize," he worries, the red light of his eyes dimming as he narrows them.

She softens her gaze and gives him a wink for reassurance. That seems to help alleviate his fears, his tense, hiked wings slumping to skim the floor.

Marcy rests her free hand on his shoulder to balance herself as she moves her lips against his palm. He is hesitant to reciprocate at first, his tongue retreating each time she playfully taunts him, unsure how to react to her intrusion.

She takes her time teaching him, guiding his lips with a gentle, loving pace, one that he picks up easily once he sheds his apprehension. It's not long after that he's moaning faintly and falls into an enjoyable, steady rhythm.

Licking at her lips, he grows more fevered, increasing the pace beyond what she originally set. His fingers clamp around her cheeks like a mask, his tongue delving deeper with clumsy enthusiasm as his confidence grows.

Oh, he's loving this.

He swirls his tongue inside her mouth, expanding his own to consume the entirety of her lips and chin. Slathering her with his saliva, it's clear he's lost quite a bit of his control.

Marcy nips at his overzealous tongue, forcing him to draw it back. He tenses bashfully, softening his tight hold.

Giggling against him, she brings her lips back to his, resuming the rhythm she started with, one not so frenzied and wooden.

He easily gets carried away, she muses.

Both her palms are now resting on Asta's shoulders, using the leverage to lift her hips, pulling off his cock until only the tip is inside. She locks her hands behind his neck, startling when he pinches her nipple. He can't seem to keep from groping her breasts, clearly his favorite part of her body. It's beginning to become her favorite, too.

He rolls the nipple between his thumb and middle finger, eliciting a groan from deep within her lungs, which he happily consumes.

Marcy leans back, sliding down his entire shaft until she's bouncing on his knot. His wispy tendrils lick her G-spot as they work themselves deeper inside her.

"Marcy," he breathes, his usually velvety voice coming out hoarse. "You feel incredible."

She nods lazily to mirror the sentiment, continuing to grind herself against his cock at a tortuously slow pace. Her eyes slam shut each time she accepts him to the hilt, the knot at his base growing in size with each pass. Chest pressing against his, she pulls him tighter, increasing the speed of her gyrations while her tongue ravages his in a heated dance.

His fully hardened girth strains at her entrance, bending and molding to fill as much of her as he can. The arms attached to his torso anchor her in place, and his lashes flutter.

Marcy glances up at him, forehead creased in question. His fingers flex against the dips of her waist, begging for permission.

He wants more.

Resting her cheek on his shoulder, she hums her approval.

"Tell me if it becomes too much, my little lamb," he says, tucking a stray lock of hair behind her ear.

There is not much Asta could do that Marcy wouldn't ardently agree to without a second thought. Especially now that she's drowning in him like a lovesick fool. While she enjoyed taking the lead, she knows he wants to be the one giving her pleasure.

Without allowing her a moment to gather herself, Asta hoists her up and off his cock in a single, steady movement, then drops her back down.

Tears build in her eyes, nails digging into his feathers as he brutally pounds her on top of his cock. The wet *slapping* sound of their bodies colliding eclipses her intensifying moans. The angle he uses to glide inside her sends bolts of crackling pleasure through her every nerve ending.

His hands cup her rear cheeks, tilting her ass forward. The new position allows her to roll herself against his quivering knot, providing her own hypersensitive clit much-needed relief. She screams his name into the void of his mouth, her words muffled to near silence.

Lustful hands seize the opportunity to knead her breasts and ass, his mouth swallowing her every mewl and scream of ecstasy, claiming them as his own.

Seconds away from climax, Marcy's back seizes, her thighs clamping against his touch. The building pressure is almost too much to bear. She needs nothing other than to come around him.

But before she can finish, Asta yanks her off him.

Vision blurry, she stares at him, dazed. Her legs dangle over the drenched bed sheets, disoriented by the denied orgasm.

He peels his hand from her mouth, saliva dripping between them to slop onto the bed. Her chest heaves, gulping down air as he carries her toward the room's floor-to-ceiling windows.

"What are you doing?" she asks, wiping her wet lips with the back of her hand.

Asta chuckles. The abundant lights from the festival below come into view as they near the window.

Marcy's stomach flips with nerves when Asta lowers her to the ground. Her feet pad the chilled marble, her back to Asta.

With the tip of his wings, he traces a line down the indent of her spine. When he reaches her lower back, he presses her into the glass.

"I thought this might be more exhilarating," he says, hooking her knee in the crook of his arm and lifting her leg.

She nearly faints at the sight of her bare breasts pressed against the window, completely visible to everyone at the festival below. The pane is spider-webbed with frost, but the haze obscures nothing.

"T-the people—" she stammers, her ears reddening.

"Are not real, remember?" he says, gesturing to the crowd. "I can make them disappear, if you would like."

Her heated cheeks practically sizzle against the glass, but a grin forms on her lips. "No, it's alright."

The initial shock may have been unpleasant, but she finds herself not *totally* opposed to the idea of exhibitionism. In fact, she actually finds it a little arousing. A part of her wishes she could see what their lewd position looks like from below. She is curious if she looks to be as drowned in lust as she feels.

"As you wish, my little lamb," Asta whispers, pushing himself closer.

He guides her leg to the side, persuading her hips to shift back against him. A full body flush paints her skin, and she spreads her palms over the window to cool herself down.

"From this position, my knot should fit," he says under his breath, almost as if reassuring himself.

She certainly hopes it can.

Slowly, he drags two fingers between her aching folds, spreading her entrance to assess her.

Marcy drags her teeth over her lip, tempted to demand he just shove it in.

"Well? Will it fit?"

One of Asta's mouthed hands presses against her core, the tongue crawling its way between her legs. If he had a face, he'd be smirking as he says, "I assure you, it will fit."

He teases the tip of his cock at her opening, running the pointed head up and down her slick seam. Her lips part, bending into him in a bid for more contact.

"Make another," Marcy says as a command rather than a suggestion.

Asta's masks slow, but he doesn't question her, creating another phallic cluster of tendrils, just as he did the first. He appears excited, but slightly apprehensive of her request.

She snorts a laugh, dragging the ring with the newly created cock to her face. This one appears to be looser in its spiral, the blue color more muted.

It must be less sensitive.

"You said you weren't concerned with your own satisfaction, but I am. I want you to feel good, too. So let me do this for you," she says, unable to expressly voice her intentions. Even while being nude against a window, it's still somehow too humiliating to say out loud.

With what sounds like an anxious gulp, he nods his rings. "That would please me greatly," he says, pushing his lower body forward to meet the ring at her pelvis.

With a tentative thrust, he plunges inside her with no resistance, her body more than willing to receive him. Excitement flutters inside her, and a soft moan breaks free. He slips in a little further, his knot testing her entrance.

Swiping her hair to the side, Asta holds it back while brushing the loose strands away from her face. At first, she believes it's because he thinks she can't see, but when she notices his masks tilt attentively, she realizes it's so *he* can see *her* better.

"Can I keep moving?" he asks, careful not to tug on her hair.

The corners of her lips lift, the gentle kindness in his question causing heat to pool where they are connected. His unassuming, solicitous demeanor is utterly irresistible. She knows how badly he wants this, yet he continues to seek her full consent.

"Always, Asta," she replies, placing a teasing peck atop his dick.

His fingertips press into her skin, like he's barely hanging on to his sanity. He whispers her name into the space between them, and a breeze from his shifting wings skitters up her back.

A stray feather dances along her shoulder, and she shivers, wiggling her hips as she clenches down on him.

That is all it takes for him to let go.

Asta pulls himself out of her entirely, sucking in a deep breath before ramming into her so hard that her breasts and stomach collide against the glass.

She mewls and rotates her hips, craving more. The soft, bouncy texture of his cock makes even the roughest thrusts feel heavenly, the friction drawing out every ounce of pleasure her body has to give.

His ring grazes her ass, his knot working her open while his clenched fingers pull her deeper. Grunting and panting in a subdued, growling voice, he pumps with abandon, losing himself in bliss.

Intent on making him unravel, Marcy wraps her lips around the rounded points of his new appendage, licking at the smooth, bulging tendrils that slap and swipe at her cheeks. Liquid beads at the dotted openings scattered across the tips of the cylindrical shapes, splashing along her taste buds. A familiar tingle flows down her throat and into her stomach, causing her toes to curl.

She wraps her fist around his girth while tilting her pelvis to slide him in easier. Sucking and lapping at every groove and flailing tendril, she traces the underside of his shaft while jacking him with long, firm pulls. He quivers in her hands, primed and ready to burst.

He snakes a mouthed hand between her legs, taking her by surprise. The sly lips attach themselves to her clit before she can react. Words are lost in her throat, her pussy throbbing and screaming for release as he drives himself into her, desperate for his own.

Each of her moans is louder than the one before as Asta focuses on her clit, propelling her to madness as she carelessly flicks her tongue over him to return the favor.

Marcy has lost all control over herself, no longer bound by shame or fear. Her leg is up in the air, her mouth is on him like it's the last thing she'll ever taste, and her lower body presses into his hand while he plunges himself so deeply, she nearly loses vision.

"Asta, faster," she purrs, the need for release building at the base of her spine. Her insides tremble and clench down on him, reaching for that sweet release lying just ahead.

He obeys her request, adjusting himself to swipe over her G-spot, hitting it enough times to have tears streaming down her face. Her fingers claw at the glass, and she throws her hips back violently. He brushes a sensual touch over her lower back, just above her ass, which is what finally allows his knot to squeeze inside her, slipping past her pelvic bone with a *pop*.

It surprises her, but the overwhelming fullness takes her right over the edge.

Marcy screams, her knees shaking as stars explode behind her eyelids. She rides his ring as she clamps down on him, memorizing every delicious inch of the glorious cock that brings her such bliss.

She struggles for air. Choking, she repeats his name like a prayer, as though she fears he'll disappear if she stops. Pressing her chest against the frigid glass, she throws her head back, a soft whine shaping her lips into an "O". Her whole body spasms, every nerve ending drowning in pure bliss.

Her muscles turn aqueous, and the only reason she remains upright is Asta's curious, exploratory hands.

His cock grows inside her as she steadily milks him in rhythmic waves, the size of his knot locking her in place.

Humming in satisfaction, Marcy blinks slowly, her vision still a little hazy. She could stay here forever, intertwined with Asta, melting from his attentions. But it's not enough. Only when he is sated will it be.

Stroking the throbbing cock at her mouth from root to tip, she whispers over her shoulder, "Take what you need." Her words drip with lulled satisfaction.

Expecting his usual gentlemanly denial, she glides her palm over a sensitive spot near the tip of his tendrils. She smirks when they pulsate wildly, continuing to press into his grooves.

He snatches her wrists, pinning them to the glass to move them out of the way. His voice erupts as a cacophony of screams before ropes of his cum coat her entire face. He drenches her in his release. She opens her mouth wide, greedy to accept it all.

She swallows any cum that lands in her mouth, moaning as the sparkles crackle down her throat. Reveling in his flavor, her tongue searches for any liquid she may have missed around her lips.

Swaying forward, Marcy swipes her tongue over his tip, lapping up the little bit of fluid that remains. She is eager to work him until both of his cocks reach ejaculation.

"Asta," she pants. "Finish inside me."

Her voice cracks with her plea, flipping a switch inside him. He rams into her, frenzied and disconnected. He has surrendered any demure restraint, hunger taking its place. His ring slaps hard against her bottom, and she's certain it will leave a mark.

His voice grows soft, weeping, the torture of a close but unrealized release bringing him to the point of insanity.

Flexing her hips, Marcy aids his clumsy rhythm. She teases his softening dick with her mouth, the aftershocks of her own orgasm squeezing him while he climbs to his.

"My little lamb," he groans. An unearthly cry rips from his chest as he buries himself to the hilt, filling Marcy with his thick release. His snug knot seals her entrance, and her stomach bows out as she reaches capacity.

He begins to remove himself, seeing that her body is at its limit, but she leans back against him in protest.

"No," she huffs, "I want it all."

Asta shivers. His lower wings wrap around her ankles as his hands caress her abdomen. He presses the slight bulge of her stomach, teasing the skin with his fingertips.

With one final, pained groan, his rings compress, the tight circles spinning faster than Marcy has seen them. They expand as he finally relaxes, breath returning to normal.

"I won't be able to remove myself as long as..." Asta mumbles while tracing her hip bone. His voice is vacant, reeling from the magnitude of the height he fell from.

She'd rather stay like this, connected to him at the deepest level and surrounded by the warmth of his body. But she knows it must eventually come to an end.

"Only if you promise to lie down with me afterward," Marcy whispers, stretching against him.

He hums, the tail end coming out high-pitched. "I don't sleep, so that's not possible. I apologize."

She snorts, grinning. "I meant for cuddling. Have you never seen a couple cuddle?"

"I have, but I can't guarantee I'll be any good at it." The shyness in his voice swells her heart.

"Let's try anyway, okay?" she says, attempting to wiggle away from him. As expected, she's completely stuck. Her feet dangle in the air, inches from the ground.

Chortling, Asta slowly frees himself. After leisurely working her off of his knot, his load pours out of her and onto the floor below her feet, catching on the inside of her thighs to mix with the remnants of her own climax.

The sound the liquid makes as it hits the ground is extraordinarily vulgar, making Marcy blush deeply.

Glancing over her shoulder, she offers a shy smile. "We made quite a mess."

"I don't mind," Asta drawls, heat lingering in his gaze. His pupils draw lines over her nude body, admiring her reddening skin that flushes deeper once she notices him staring.

He seems to be entranced by the image of his release scattered across her chest and thighs. There's an edge of possessiveness in the way his blunt fingers dig deeper into her hips. However, none of it is rooted in sexual desire. Each gentle stroke of her skin is rooted in adoration, a yearning to hold her simply for the sake of it.

It's a sensation she could get used to. The hollow pit inside her chest floods with warmth from Asta's enveloping affection.

Once she is back on the ground, Marcy shifts her weight from one foot to the other, and with a hint of reluctance says, "We should probably clean ourselves up. Before everything, um, *dries*." She can't meet his gaze or force herself to say anything more.

Asta sighs, insinuating that he shares her reluctance. Nevertheless, he replies, "As you wish."

With a leisurely snap of his fingers, any evidence of what just transpired vanishes.

She startles, frozen in shock, while a single brow creases her forehead.

"I can alter my own matter. Never mind the mess, now," he says cheekily, drawing her to his chest.

Her back is enveloped by feathers as she lifts her chin to his masks. "Ever the gentleman," she says, pulling the fox mask down to plant a soft kiss on the snout.

While initially relieved at her sudden cleanliness, she doesn't antici-pate the feeling of emptiness now that he is no longer inside her. Her heart yearns to be one with him, filled in every way possible.

She stifles her crude thoughts with another peck to his mask and hopes he doesn't notice her disappointment at no longer being covered in his essence.

Asta releases a pleased exhale, none the wiser. He strokes the span of her stomach with loving intention, seemingly unable to get enough of her skin. She can understand. The tingling sensation of his nimble fingertips is a soothing comfort, the prickles of electricity letting her know he's there.

Her head dips into his chest as she continues to pepper lazy kisses along his mask. Her knees wobble as she turns toward him, completely losing the ability to stand.

"Would you like to rest in bed?" he asks, stroking her hair.

Marcy nods, her heart bursting with reverence. "I'd love that."

Chapter 13

Astamesiophelous

Never in his entire existence did Astamesiophelous think he would lie with another being, let alone a *human.* But while sprawled across silken bed sheets with Marcy tucked beneath his arm, he understands why the gods forbid such relationships.

Humanity can be cruel. During his tenure as the Evaluator, he has witnessed every negative scenario imaginable. From bitter divorces, years-long revenge plots, or stealing from the less fortunate, the depravity of humankind knows no limits. Those experiences, however, while horrid and brutal, pale in comparison to the all-encompassing deluge of romantic devotion.

He used to think the humans he evaluated were foolish to risk everything for a lover, especially if it resulted in their demise. But now, it all makes sense.

Asta would brave every complicated aspect of the human experience if it meant he could love Marcy for just one second longer.

She hums against his chest, cheek pressing into the bone that holds his torso together. He runs his fingers through her long, sandy colored hair, getting them tangled in the knots.

"It would be easier with a brush, you know," she murmurs, voice gruff with sleep.

He stills against her scalp. "I don't know what that is. Can you describe it to me?"

He's seen an endless number of human tools and inventions through the memories of those he's evaluated, but he never took the time to truly examine them. It seemed unnecessary.

Pressing her finger to the center of his chest, Marcy traces a shape against the feathers. "Square at the top, with little bristles poking out. *Soft* bristles." She draws a skinny "U" shape. "Then, there's a handle at the bottom so you can hold it easily."

A brush instantly appears in his hand, the manifestation a little cruder than he intended. Nevertheless, it will work.

"So can you make anything appear?" she asks, sighing when Asta starts running the brush through her tresses.

He drags it down the strands of her hair, careful not to tug.

"Yes and no. I'm allowed to create anything that will aid in my evaluation," he explains. "But the power is not my own. I request the changes from the gods. Anything relating to my own body, however, is mine alone to manipulate."

Rolling her head to the side, she gives him more access to her scalp, happily rubbing her feet together beneath the covers with every swipe of the brush.

"Do they know you created a brush, then?"

He chuckles, and with a mischievous lilt he says, "No."

"Will they find out about…?"

She doesn't need to finish her question for Asta to know what she's implying.

"They will, eventually. I will be reprimanded for the favor I have shown you, but since I am nearing the end of my existence, they will likely be lenient."

Marcy's expression sours. "Reprimand you how?"

Explaining the cosmic horrors the gods may use to punish him would only result in upsetting her further, so he chooses not to answer her question.

"Do not concern yourself with such things," he says with a laugh. "All they care about right now is that I evaluate your soul."

Being reminded of the reason she is here in the first place makes her muscles tense, a frown carving deep lines into her cheeks. As much as Asta would like to spend eternity lying here with her, it is not possible. All things must come to an end.

Marcy lies in silence with a grave look on her face. He continues to drag the brush through her hair, pulling the knots free until it's completely smooth. She is stunning no matter how she looks, but he finds himself partial to her with her hair down — captivated by how the locks fall against her bare back, shining like velvet.

Marcy presses her lips together while tightening her grip on his arm. "How long do we have?"

A pang of unease stabs him in the chest, an unfamiliar feeling taking root.

"Until we witness your final memory. Then, I will have to make my decision."

She acknowledges him with a slight, melancholic nod.

"Our time together must eventually end, Marcy. You can't stay in the ethereal realm forever," he says, setting the brush aside. "I cannot control that. I apologize."

"I know," she replies, lifting her chin. "But it's hard not to feel sad about it."

He shares her sentiment. The end of their time together looms like an abyss. It feels as if they are seconds from falling off a cliff with no way to prevent it.

But he will not squander the few precious moments they have left by fretting over it.

"Let us not discuss such unfortunate things." He brushes a knuckle over her cheek, coaxing a smile from her tight lips. "Tell me about your happiest times, ones that we did not get to see in your memories. I would like to know more about what brings you joy."

She sticks out her tongue in thought, trying to hide her excitement. "Fine, but I get to ask you a question first, okay?"

"Of course," he says, elated to see some of the sparkle returning to her eyes.

"Well, it's more of a favor, but I'd like you to teach me how to pronounce your name. Your *full name*." She places a special emphasis on the last words.

"Why? It is complicated, and you have no need to use it," he challenges. A human has never pronounced his name correctly, hence why he gave himself the nickname.

She pulls her lips into a thin line. "I… I really like you, Asta, and I'd like to take the time to show that to you."

Her explanation is simple, yet it is no simple thing for him. He never imagined a mortal taking the *time* to learn his full name, and it excites him in a way he does not know how to describe. Perhaps this is love. He has acted as a conduit of the sensation through the memories of others, but even with his newly erupting emotions, he has never experienced it first-hand before.

Love.

He may not know exactly what love is, but it is indubitable to him that he loves *her*.

"Okay, I shall teach you," he relents with a pat on her back. "And I will not be offended if you fail."

She smirks, propping her chin atop her fists. "I'm not going to fail. I was just nervous the first time you said it. Now, try me."

While her taunt is convincing, it takes her an extraordinary amount of time to grasp the fifth and sixth syllables. Although frustrated, she persists. Expression pinched in concentration, she is intent on succeeding and proving herself right.

"Astamesio-fel-is."

"Close."

She clears her throat, embarrassed.

Asta repeats his entire name back to her: "Astamesiophelous."

"*Astamesiophelous*," she echoes correctly.

The sound of his full name on her lips is erotic enough that he almost orgasms. He is grateful that his dematerialized genitals are tucked away inside his rings. To prematurely ejaculate in front of Marcy for a second time would be much too mortifying.

But Marcy quickly catches on to his aroused squirming, licking her lips lasciviously. "*Astamesiophelous,*" she repeats in a singsong voice. "Astamesiophelous. Astamesiophelous—"

Slapping a hand over her mouth, flames lick his masks as he says, "P-please stop. You have succeeded."

She chuckles while prying his hand away from her lips. Her smile stretches up to her eyes as she flops on top of him, sighing. "Fine. But I find your reaction to hearing your name very cute."

'Cute' has never been a word used to describe him. He likes it.

"By the way, where did you get your name?" she asks. "Did you choose it?"

She requested *one* question before sharing her happiest memories with him. She has now asked multiple questions, plus a favor, but he refrains from pointing that out.

"I did not name myself. The gods named me," he says, the origins of his existence a long-forgotten memory. "My name means 'made of stars'."

"How fitting," she mutters and slides her fingertips over his skin, tracing the dimly connected constellations that span across his arms.

While he'd normally allow her to touch him to her heart's content, he longs to ask a question of his own. "I fulfilled your request, now you must fulfill mine," he says, petting the length of her hair. "Tell me one of your happiest moments, no matter how small."

Her eyebrows lift in thought before she says, "Okay. I have a few, if that's alright."

"Of course it is," he responds, skimming the curvature of her cheekbone with his thumb.

Marcy barely makes it halfway through a story about her strawberry jam winning first prize at a fair before her eyelids start to droop. The rise and fall of her chest grows weightier with each word.

Her mood is certainly improved, and Asta is not surprised by her exhaustion. Spending this long in the ethereal realm is bound to take its toll on her, eventually. He has never seen fatigue like this, since he has never spent this much time with a human. Ever. It usually only takes him a handful of memories to complete an evaluation.

It makes him wonder why Marcy needs to be evaluated at all. The question looms no matter how many times he replays her memories, none of which paint her as despicable in any way. She's made human errors, but nothing grave enough to warrant an evaluation, surely.

Her body relaxes, her warm skin kissing his own as she is lulled into sleep. All the while, his curiosity evolves until it's nearly unmanageable.

Asta knows there is only one memory left to witness, which causes a sinking feeling to fester inside him. Whatever the memory is, it *must* be the reason Marcy was sent to him. In his millennia of experience, every human who is sent through evaluation holds dark secrets that cannot be ignored, despite any goodness they may have.

Asta wraps his arm around her waist and pulls her closer. Gently, he presses the lips of his mask into her cheek.

To complete his purpose, he must witness the memory.

Even if it is dark enough to swallow him whole.

Chapter 14

Astamesiophelous

A woman sits on a couch, her light-brown hair tied sloppily into a low bun. Her chin rests on the heel of her palm, and the yellow dress she wears is wrinkled and dirty. On a nearby table, a clear glass sits atop a coaster, the remnants of a dark liquid pooling at the bottom.

The front door opens, revealing a sign hanging from it that reads 'Merry Christmas' as it bangs against the wall. In walks a man wearing a sleek, dark blue suit. His hair is slicked back with so much gel it looks solid. He scowls at the woman the moment his shoes cross the threshold, dropping his briefcase to the ground with a loud *thump*.

"Why don't I smell dinner, Marce?" the man sneers, pulling his thin lips into a mocking smile. "You can't drink the days away anymore. You've got to make yourself useful."

Instead of looking in his direction, the woman continues to stare at the wall. Her eyes are lifeless, glazed over to the point where she could be mistaken for a doll.

She doesn't flinch when the man slams the door shut, loosening the tie around his neck with his free hand.

"Are you even fucking listening to me?" he shouts, unlatching the gold watch around his wrist. He tosses it onto the sideboard near the entryway, dropping his head with a huff. "You're just like your father, a worthless—"

"I know Angela's pregnant."

The man freezes, his skin turning a ghostly shade of white. Whatever bravado he walked in with is gone, stomped to smithereens as the woman finally lifts her cold gaze to meet his.

"I don't know what—"

"Don't act stupid, David. I'm not an idiot," she says calmly, her words slightly slurred. She scrubs her face with her palm. The bags under her tired eyes are a dull gray, covered by thick makeup to hide the angry purple and red tones there. "You don't even try to hide it, toting her around town like she's your prized pony."

The man crosses his arms defiantly, glaring down his nose at her. "She likes being around me, you know that."

"She's sixteen!" the woman shouts. Jumping up from the couch, she knocks over her glass, spilling the meager contents onto the carpet. "What the hell is wrong with you? I babysat her! We were in her parents' wedding!"

Crossing the narrow space between them, the woman points a finger at him, her hands trembling. "It's *your* baby, David. Admit it," she growls under her breath.

Raising his arm, the man smacks away her accusatory finger. With his other hand, he grabs her wrist, yanking her forward until their noses nearly touch.

"And? So what, Marcy? At least she's not a goddamn drunkard and a thief. That pretty little thing enjoys the duties *you* neglect. And as a bonus, this broad can actually give me a son," he spits out, the subtle smirk playing at his lips suggesting he enjoys this exchange. More precisely, he enjoys watching the woman unravel before him.

Struggling against his hold, the woman attempts a step backward, her expression melting into fear. The dynamic of their argument subtly shifts, almost imperceptibly, but the woman is acutely aware of it. It is a situation she appears familiar with.

"You're sick," she breathes, her entire body shaking like an autumn leaf.

The man lifts his free hand, laughing when she recoils and squeezes her eyes shut.

"And you're just an annoying pair of walking breasts. Not even nice ones at that." The man grabs the back of her head, forcing her to meet his gaze directly. "You're a terrible wife who can't fuck right, can't bear children, can't cook, can't clean, can't even *look pretty* for her husband when he gets home."

Her eyes dart back and forth between his, like a rabbit caught in a snare. "David, you know it's not my fault. My womb… My father—"

"'*Not my fault*'?" he snaps. Eyes widening with rage, his pupils almost obscure his irises. "And it's not *my* fault God gave me a defective wife!" Shoving the woman to the ground, he stands over her, his expression savage. "Oh boo-hoo, daddy hurt you. Stop acting like a victim, Marcy. I'm in my mid-forties with no children. Have you ever stopped to think about how that makes *me* look? About *my* happiness? About anything other than *yourself*?"

Tears spill from the woman's eyes as she cowers below him, trying and failing to wipe them away with the back of her hand. "So, your solution was to prey on a child? We're married, David. The church will not look kindly on you."

With a huff, he looks over his shoulder to where he tossed his watch. A ceramic pot sits behind a miniature photo frame, housing what looks to be a black and white image with concentric circles.

"What am I left with, then?" His dark eyes snap back to the woman on the floor. "*You?*"

"David, I—"

The woman is cut off abruptly.

"I don't need to be reminded of your failures, *or* you," he barks, taking the ceramic pot in one hand. "I *finally* have a baby on the way, and an obedient woman who dotes on me every chance she gets. And don't kid yourself, the people of our church will be more than happy to see me rid of you. All you're known for is puking in the pews and skipping ladies' bible study. You won't be missed." Satisfaction thrums through his voice, like how someone might gloat after finding a long-forgotten treasure. He revels at seeing this woman in despair, his cruel grin causing lines to wrinkle around his heartless eyes.

Recognizing the object in the man's hand, the woman gasps, her face contorting in horror. She staggers to her feet, reaching for it in desperation. "No, David, no!"

After briefly inspecting the pot, the man lifts his arm and launches it to the ground, inches from his feet. The ceramic shatters on impact, dust wafting up and into the woman's face after she drops to the floor in an attempt to save it from destruction.

She coughs uncontrollably, waving her hand to dispel the dust as she hoarsely screams, "David! What have you done?" The agony in her voice could make a statue weep. As the man's actions finally sink in, she realizes the extent of his maliciousness.

Then comes her rage.

Lunging at the man, the woman grabs the collar of his shirt. She shakes him violently, but he doesn't look distressed. In fact, he looks nothing but pleased.

"How *could* you?" she screams. Sobs catch in her throat as moisture drips from her eyes and nose. "Why? Why are you being so cruel? I did my best for you!"

With a single shove, he overpowers her, letting out a smug laugh as she once again falls to the ground. He kneels over her, pinning her wrists above her head. "God, your screeching is unbearable."

His hands move from her wrists to her neck. His grip forms a collar around her throat as he squeezes her fragile skin. He rocks his body forward until the majority of his weight is concentrated at her throat, no doubt a familiar position.

The woman unsuccessfully gasps for air, but all that escapes is a hissing sound. While there is fear evident in her tearful eyes, there is also acceptance. A peace.

She believes she deserves this.

"The church will definitely forgive a *widower*, won't they Marce?" he asks with a sadistic laugh. "Especially when they find out that it was your barren womb that drove you crazy. That you drunkenly trashed every memento from your sad little life before choking yourself to death with your darling husband's belt. Or a rope. I haven't decided yet."

The man squeezes his palms tighter. Eyes filled with pure evil, he can't seem to control his near maniacal laughter.

It's at this moment that the woman realizes his intention: to finally kill her.

Choking and shivering, she claws at his forearms for relief, her strength slowly fading.

"Da...vi...d." she wheezes, panicked.

"You just won't shut up, will you?" he snorts. A vein protrudes from his forehead, and his fists clench so tightly that the knuckles try to burst from his skin.

The woman's hands fall to her sides, limp, fingers twitching.

"God, I fucking hate you."

The man's words summon a minuscule amount of self-preservation in her, which is quickly fueled by her intense rage. With a final dredge of energy, she feels along the ground, her palms slicing open on the tiny, shattered pieces of the ceramic. Running her fingers over a large shard, she grips it tightly despite the sharp edges cutting into to her skin. Swinging as hard as she can, she spears the man's neck with the ceramic.

The shard makes direct contact, splitting the skin with astonishing ease. Crimson pours from his neck as he frantically tries to stanch the flow. But there is nothing he can do. Nothing that can save him.

Crumbling like a rag doll, the man slumps forward, on top of the woman. His eyes are spread wide as his life force continues to spill, the once fiery orbs now devoid of life.

Beneath him, the woman is unable to regain her breath. Instead, she wheezes a few huffs of air before her face softens, leaving a permanent look of sadness etched into her delicate features.

Silence.

The room falls into a haunting chill as the lingering dust begins to settle around the bodies. They are pressed together begrudgingly, like opposing magnets.

Asta is left staring, the rings of his head motionless.

A heavy tear falls from each of his masks, sliding down the smooth surfaces before dropping to the feathers of his chest. For the first time in his entire existence, Asta cries. Grief doesn't even *begin* to encompass the heartbreak ripping him to shreds. It is painful, both inside and out. Enough to make him feel ill.

It suddenly dawns on him that he is experiencing the full breadth of sadness, this *ache,* without a human vessel. Emotions aren't usually this strong when he's the only witness — or rather, they *weren't* this strong.

Everything is strange. The feelings are foreign. They're…

Human.

"Asta…?" a voice gingerly calls behind him.

Alarmed, Asta whirls around, tufts of his feathers scattering into the air around him. His chest seizes, and his wings flap with his panicked anxiety.

Marcy.

Chapter 15

Astamesiophelous

Marcy sits atop the heap of pillows, covers pulled up to her chest. She looks petrified, a queasy dullness painting her skin a ghoulish green.

"I am so sorry, Marcy… I could not help myself." Asta's voice is timid, his body language cornered and defensive. He knows he should not have looked, especially without Marcy, but his newfound devotion to her has more power over him than he'd like to admit.

Despite Marcy's visible anguish, she does not shed a single tear. Her face is as hard as stone. The space between her brows is furrowed so tightly that it looks like it hurts.

"I knew you'd be curious about how my life ended. It was unfair of me to keep it from you, especially considering…" She uses her hand to motion between the two of them.

Pulling the covers to her chin, her gaze drifts uneasily about the room, as if searching for what to say. "I didn't want you to be mad at me."

Asta's rings recoil in shock, his feathers pressing flush against his torso.

"*Mad?*" he echoes.

Marcy nods with a long, drawn-out sigh. "I killed my husband and don't feel any remorse over it," she explains, shaking her head. "I couldn't let him have the *one thing* I desperately wanted in my life, so I *had* to end it, no matter the consequences."

Her voice wavers, but her resolve remains absolute. She will not mourn the man, and she has no intention of seeking forgiveness or absolution.

Although it goes against the very purpose of his existence, Asta admires her for this.

"I am not mad at you."

Her gaze flicks to him in puzzlement. "How can you not be? I tried to hide the fact that I killed someone, something that guarantees my soul will be damned — or whatever horrible fate awaits me." Her shoulders shake, not in sorrow, but in fury. The sheets fall to her lap as the emotion overtakes her. "I let you believe I was someone worth pitying. That all my previous mistakes were anomalies, excusable when overshadowed by the tragedy that was my life. In reality, I was consumed by hatred and jealousy in my final moments, which I channeled into a determination to kill that *rotten* man."

Asta's wings flare with indignation. He moves to firmly cup Marcy's face in his palm, forcing her to keep her roving eyes on him. He refuses to let her look away. He has had enough of her self-deprecation.

"It is against the rules for me to tell you this, but I suppose I have disregarded so many others that it hardly matters now," he begins, giving her a compassionate look as her dark pupils swell in humiliation. "Not every human is evaluated. *You* were sent to me."

Marcy tilts her head, but his tight grip on her chin prevents any further movement.

"I don't understand," she says. "I thought all souls are judged?"

"They are, to a certain degree, but most human souls are discernibly black or white in nature, which does not require further scrutiny. They were either good, or they were bad. And that's all there is to it."

Pressing the tip of her tongue to the roof of her mouth, she mulls over his words.

"I take it that I didn't fall into either category, then?" she eventually asks, a bit unsettled.

"Correct," he replies, brushing his thumb over her lips. "Life isn't always so simple. Human beings are complex. Sometimes, the line between 'good' and 'bad' is so thin that I, the Evaluator, am tasked with investigating further, ensuring that the mortal's soul is bound for the correct place. Those being evaluated are never supposed to know the delicate line they walk when I present them with their memories."

Marcy's lips purse, tugging them away from Asta's touch.

"I think I understand … If I knew it's uncommon for a soul to need evaluation, and that I was on the cusp of either reconstruction or reincarnation, I might try to sway your opinion of me. Push you toward the outcome I'd prefer…"

"Most humans need little reason to beg for a gentler fate, but remaining unaware of how abnormal it is to have lived a truly morally ambiguous life certainly helps with their honesty," he says with a light chuckle.

Marcy doesn't smile or acknowledge his levity. "You get to decide what happens to me, after this."

"I do. It is my purpose."

Her eyes soften, glazed over in downtrodden gloom. "I killed my husband because I didn't want him to have a baby, which I could never have myself. I wanted to die, but I wanted to take him down with me. It was not self-defense, and it wasn't altruistic. I was selfish — I *am* selfish," she murmurs in a wobbly voice. "Well, what do you think I deserve, Asta? After everything you've seen." Her lip quivers as she gestures to the disappearing scene of her last moments.

His rings dip to the side, bewildered. "What a silly question. You will be reincarnated."

"Wait, what?" she blurts, befuddled.

His feathers ruffle as he admits, "I've become human to a fault, and there is no way for me to go back to the apathetic creature I pretended to be for so long. I adore you, Marcy. I would never let you be reconstructed. Ever."

Chapter 16

Marcy

Huffing, she's not strong enough to force Asta's hand away. Seeing her desperate struggle, he quickly releases his grip, tugging his arm against his chest as though he touched a flame.

Guilt slams into Marcy's chest, but it doesn't matter. She sinned. There is nothing that can save her. Nothing that *should* save her.

"No, Asta, you can't spare me because of that!" she exclaims, stomping from the bed with the sheets still wrapped around her body. Her breath is shallow as she frantically searches for her clothing. "I spent my whole life believing that the wicked will be punished and the pious will be rewarded — you *can not* let me be an exception to that. Otherwise, everything I devoted my life to, *suffered* for, would have been *for nothing*. I know what I deserve, and I was wrong to let myself get carried away."

Despite his size, Asta somehow manages to make himself look small. His wings retract, and his floating rings slow their orbit.

"Marcy—"

"No!" she shouts, pulling her dress over her head in aggravation. She clamps her palms over her eyes, worried that if she looks at him now, she'll lose her nerve. "I murdered someone. It doesn't matter *why* I did it — I still broke one of the Ten Commandments. You of all people should know that I don't deserve the grace you seem intent on giving me. You *saw* what I did."

Asta floats in silence, either too afraid to speak or allowing her the time to calm down. Both of those possibilities trouble her.

Marcy inhales sharply before spreading her fingers. She peers through the opening, but all she can see is the bright red glow of Asta's eyes.

"I refused my wifely duties, couldn't bear children, stole from the congregation, lied, drank, and was not obedient to my husband *or* Father. And that's *on top* of committing murder. I…" Although she tries to halt the burgeoning tears, to not show such a sorry side of herself, she is powerless to stop the torrent. Sobs burst from her mouth as her fingers twist into the hair covering her face.

"I hate myself." Nails dig into her skin, red, angry lines forming on her forehead as she curls her fingers. "I want to be punished, Asta. I want to be freed from this anguish, from a life that's only caused me pain. I want my soul to be torn apart so no part of me is forced to exist again in any lifetime, ever."

When she drops her hands, her vision is blurred from the tears streaming down the smile lines of her cheeks and onto her dress. "It's funny, really, I actually looked forward to eternal damnation — at least the biblical description of it. The idea of my soul suffering from physical pain rather than meeting my loved ones in heaven was oddly comforting. It's something I *know* I can endure. The emotional toll, however," she shakes her head, "is too much. No one wants me around, not in this life or the next. I can't let myself be disappointed again."

Marcy wipes the corners of her eyes with the heel of her palm, then looks directly at Asta as she says, "I want to be *gone.*"

The words echo, leaving an icy chill in the once joy-filled space. Asta remains still, eyes unblinking. Only the sound of Marcy's heavy pants fill the silence as she waits for him to respond. If he even will. She voiced what's been bothering her this entire time… but she thought she would feel better after admitting it.

Even without a face, Marcy can tell he is despondent with the way his wings droop low.

"Asta…? Say something," she starts, gripping the skirt of her dress tightly. "I've enjoyed my time with you, you know that, but—"

"*I* want you here, Marcy," he whispers. "I want you around. In every life."

Glowing tears drip from the eye holes of his bull and fox masks, falling to the ground in illuminated puddles. There is a hitch to his voice, and a miserable aura surrounds them both. Powerful and captivating.

He hovers closer to her but keeps a cautious arm's length away.

"There is not a single reality, timeline, or universe where I would not choose to reincarnate you," he laments, a hand pressed to his chest. "I could never rob the universe of your soul, of any *scrap* of your essence."

Marcy rubs her lips together, grinding the heel of her foot against the ground. "You're only saying that because I'm the first human you met after your emotions became so strong. I could have been anyone else, and you would've felt the same. There's nothing special about me other than I appeared in the right place at the right time."

She doesn't need to see him to know that her words wound him.

In a hushed, somber voice, he replies, "That's not true at all."

"Isn't it?" she presses. Crossing her arms, her jaw clenches. "If I allow you to make this decision, with your emotions in their current state, I feel like I'd be manipulating you for my own gain. I'd loathe that."

She startles when a hand appears behind her back, pressing her into Asta, face-first. As she attempts to extract herself from the plumage of his chest, an arm wraps around her waist, pulling her back in.

When Marcy looks up, she sees that Asta's masks have taken on new expressions, the eyes appearing downturned and distressed. Shining tears fall from each mask, ice cold as they drip onto her skin.

"You are," his words hitch as he trembles, "the *only* human who did not demand I change from my true form. You treated me like a person: you asked me about myself, learned to pronounce my name, fed me homemade desserts, danced with me, and allowed me to experience happy events from your memories. All things a being like me could never have on their own. For the first time in my existence, a human wanted to share their joy with me. I was elated."

Running her fingers through his dampened feathers, she tries to gently soothe the ache she hears in his voice.

Tugging her tighter, he continues, "I wish I could accurately express how isolating it was to spend thousands of millennia alone. Where every human I came across wanted to be rid of me. Developing human emotions is a defect of my design, something I should never wish to have and have been told to abhor." He shifts his wings so his feathers envelope her completely, cocooning her in his comforting warmth. "Yet, ever since I met you, all I wanted is to feel the full spectrum of human emotions. The sorrow, the joy, the jealousy, the anger… All of it, the good and the bad."

Marcy's heart breaks for him. She regrets her cruel words, even if she believes them. Despite her best efforts to challenge her internal turmoil, her feelings remain the same.

Tongue darting between her lips, she wets them before she speaks. "Asta, I don't want to exist anymore. I fear that in my next life, and all those after, I'll just end up suffering again." She drops her head, pressing her forehead into his feathers. "I don't have it in me to carry on, especially if I won't have another chance to make this decision in the future. My soul is burdened with too many sins, and I want to be released."

Asta brings his fingers to the top of her head, drawing circles along her scalp. He no longer weeps, and affection softens his words.

"Marcy, my love, I have witnessed deplorable acts from millions of souls, all with their own unique story. Many of the souls capable of such acts were horrible people, but you are not one of them." He tilts her head up to his masks. She lowers her eyelids, looking up at him through her damp eyelashes. "You were not a bad wife or a bad person, and you owed no one your body for procreation. The people who were supposed to love and protect you harmed you instead, degrading your sense of self until you became convinced you don't deserve an iota of compassion."

Opening her mouth to refute his statement, Marcy only lets out a single squeak before Asta presses his finger to her lips.

"You have done bad things and lived to regret them, but it does not strip you of your core values. You are not your worst moments," he pleads. "Cruelty in the universe is absolute, and in your life, you were on the receiving end. Believe me, as a being who has witnessed all the joys and horrors humanity is capable of, the things you claim are 'sins' have little meaning in the afterlife."

Asta's feathers ruffle when the corners of Marcy's mouth begin to turn upwards, a ghost of a smile on her lips. But it is not born from happiness.

"I murdered my husband, Asta. That has meaning."

"If it were as black and white as you seem to think, we would have never met," he says, bothered by her continued refusal. "It is my responsibility to evaluate you and make the decision, not yours. You believe you need to be judged, and perhaps that is why you were sent here. But I disagree with you."

The tears glistening in the corners of her eyes fade, leaving a glassy look of indifference.

"You shouldn't care so much. I was nice to you, that's all," she mumbles. "Why can't you let me go?"

"Because *I don't want to*," he snaps. His rings form hundreds of little hands that tighten around her body in an embrace. Every one of them tingles, sparks snapping across her skin.

"The people in your life took everything from you, but you were still kind until they broke you. Your body could not bear fruit, yet you gave your love and care to the little creatures around you. The universe tortured you, gave you every reason to hate being alive," he lowers his masks to her face, brushing both of her cheeks in a kiss, "yet your vibrant spirit evoked love within a soulless creature, who is *begging* you to live."

She sighs, but a grin forms. His tantrum is as sweet as it is surprising. He is naïve, like a newborn experiencing the world for the first time. But she'd be lying if she said his pleas weren't convincing.

Never in her life did someone fight for her like this. No one took an interest beyond what was useful to them; willingly entertained her every whim; or loved and comforted her in the painful moments, even when it was difficult. She was never shown love through her struggles, when things weren't okay and she needed it the most.

Maybe she….

God.

I think I love him.

Marcy grabs his fox mask, pressing her lips to his. Holding him there, she lets out a laugh. An ember of perseverance, a will to live, begins to burn.

"You are quite the romantic," she teases, biting down a wide smile. "I'm blushing."

"I mean it, Marcy. Stay," he begs. The seriousness in his tone warns her that he will not let her go so easily.

"I…. I don't know if I can."

His rings spin as he thinks, becoming flustered with urgency and exasperation. His next words stun her, and by the look of surprise in his eyes, they are a shock to him as well.

"Will you stay if I accompany you to the mortal world?"

Chapter 17

Astamesiophelous

He is gobsmacked by the suggestion he just made. So candidly, so *easily*.

Give up an eternity among the stars, creating new galaxies and other living beings, to be human? However surprised he may be at his own words, not once does he think of rescinding the offer.

Marcy's thin brows crash together, a look of admonition in her expression. "You can't do that… can you? How would that even work?"

Asta ponders the question for a moment, since he is not entirely sure, himself. These kinds of things don't happen often, if at all. Surely, the gods would be furious if they knew he was entertaining the thought.

"I am not certain how it would work for me, but I have seen what happens to lesser beings when they choose to reincarnate themselves. I suspect my energy would be added to your world's pool, then my essence dispersed among living things. I may become a part of a human, animal, or a piece of grass upon the soil," he shrugs as Marcy shakes from an incredulous laugh in his grip. "The possibilities excite me. I could reincarnate into *anything*. Although, I hope it is as a human."

Marcy wraps her arms around his neck, staying close to his masks. "There's a lot that comes with being human. This isn't a decision you should make lightly, especially when you don't even know if it's allowed."

While he understands her hesitation, it does not deter him.

"To my knowledge, there has never been an Evaluator that desired to reincarnate, so it is neither allowed nor forbidden," he explains. "And I don't intend to ask the gods' permission in the first place."

Marcy snickers. "What a rebellious thing to do, just to end up suffering like the rest of us."

She still doesn't understand the magnitude of the situation, but her naivety puts him at ease. He strokes her cheek in reverence.

"I am aware that human emotions can be a burden. That they can make a person wish to end their own life, or the lives of others. I know that some people never recover from the damage, and those who do, carry it forever." His somber tone shifts, filling with pure joy as he says, "But the unknowns are worth facing if it means the opportunity to experience the sweetest euphoria of living, isn't it?" If he had a mouth, he'd be smiling from ear to ear.

Marcy drops her gaze with a relenting sigh. "I suppose."

"Much like you, the only existence I have ever known is one filled with empty duty," he says. Running his hands down her sides, he revels in her shivered response. "But my time with you has made the millennia of loneliness feel worth it. I know this will remain true, even if my reincarnation is not as I expect. My love is with you, my little lamb, and I will follow you wherever you go."

Marcy shifts her weight, hair spilling over her shoulders as she tilts her head back in thought.

"So, you'll only reincarnate if I do?"

"Yes."

She snorts, then shakes her head. "Asta, I don't think—"

"Would you be willing to live again, knowing that somewhere, I exist? That no matter what reality or world you end up in, there will be someone who loves you with their entire being, fighting to be a part of your life?" His red eyes are wide and shining. "I'll always find you, no matter where you are or how difficult it is for me to get there, and I will carry you through the hardest times."

He's trembling, unsure of the exact cause of his nervousness but knows it's tied to however she responds to what he says next.

"I love you, Marcy. You are worth relinquishing my immortality for."

She's speechless. Her lips part, but she has no words to follow such a proclamation. Instead, a blush blooms across her nose and cheeks.

Asta steels himself for the pain of rejection. It is an emotion he has yet to feel personally, but he is prepared to confront the possibility. He has no regrets.

"I shall ask one last time: will you reincarnate if I come with you?"

Burying her face in his chest, she laughs so loud that it vibrates his feathers. He has no idea if it is *good* laughter, but he is delighted by the sound, nonetheless.

Lifting her head, Marcy's cheeks are as rosy and plump as apples, the soft smile that curves her lips reaching her eyes. There is something about her expression that Asta can't place, but the subtle change to how she leans against him warms his insides.

"Okay," she says, pecking the snout of his bull mask. "Will you stop throwing a fit if I agree to *one* more life? Then, after that, if I still don't want to live, I want to be reconstructed. How does that sound?"

"You will want to stay. I shall make sure of it," he replies with confidence.

"And if I don't, make sure you tell your angel colleagues what I want. You can't go back on this, alright?" She tries to be serious, but her giggling betrays her.

Teasing or not, Asta doesn't have the heart to tell her he has no idea who the next Evaluator will be. But he will ensure her wishes are honored, even if he disagrees with them.

"I will make sure. You have my word," he vows.

"Then I'll try again, for you," she sighs with a huff, shaking her head as though she can't believe she's agreeing to his request.

His rings vibrate with jubilation, spreading a heat that carries an abundance of ecstasy. How humorous emotions are. What he once viewed as a scourge to his existence is now something he craves, and he couldn't be happier.

He only notices that tears are once again pouring from his masks when Marcy whisks them away with a loving smile.

I will live for her, and only her.

Asta embraces her tightly, willing his immense love to flood her soul in their final moments here. It is what she deserved, all along.

The call of resolution buzzes inside of him like a swarm of bees. It has never been painful for him to release a soul, but now, the thought may as well rip him in half.

"With my decision made and your final memory witnessed," he starts gently, "It is time for us to go."

His hands shake, but he is not afraid of the unknown. Infinite possibilities lie before them, and while some may separate him from Marcy, he doesn't worry. He is certain that this is the right decision, like the gods placed this knowledge inside his being long before he understood it.

Almost as if he now knows meeting Marcy is destiny.

Fate.

He does not believe in such things, but he will. For her.

Outstretching his hand, he offers it to her. She takes it without hesitation.

Chapter 18

Marcy

With Marcy cradled in his arms, Asta allows the memory of the winter festival to fade away. Flying past the disappearing dancing figures, spires of bright light appear in front of them.

Despite the dread and anxiety swarming her gut, a spark of excitement ignites into a weak flame. She feels content. Happy even. The notion is strange, as she thought her fate was sealed the moment she realized she was dead.

Her evaluation feels like it took so long... yet it is ending all too quickly. A sensation of longing, of needing to spend just one more second with Asta, is what changed her mind. Even if she is born into a life of suffering again, she will not be alone. And that makes all the difference.

They approach a breathtaking display of bright, glowing pillars. Below each one of them is a small, gold-encrusted circle. Shadowy figures step between the beams of light, rising up and out of view until they disappear, leaving behind nothing more than sparkles that fall to coat the ground.

Asta lands beside one of the golden circles, lowering Marcy to her feet.

Her heart pounds wildly in her chest, but she does not second-guess her decision. With Asta's hand in hers, feeling the subtle tingle of his skin, she is ready to try again.

With him.

"When you are ready, we shall step into the light," he says, giddy.

She cocks her head and raises a brow. "You're not scared?"

"I am terrified. But that is what makes it exciting, yes? We do not know what's next. It could be anything."

Marcy nods, drawing in a deep, calming breath. Stepping into the light means possible misery, but it also means that, for the first time, she'll have someone with her. She will not suffer in isolation.

'You are worth relinquishing my immortality for.'

Asta's words echo in her mind, giving her the little shred of courage she needs to take her first step toward the light.

This time it will be different. This time, she will be loved.

"I think I'm ready," she says, tugging on his arm.

Following her onto the platform, they stand inches away from the pillar. A gentle buzzing rings in her ears, and her breath grows shallow. The light is much more blinding up close. It's opaque, impossible for her to look through.

She chews her lower lip, and a quiver builds in her knees.

Asta squeezes her hand, jolting her out of her worries.

"I shall be with you the entire time, Marcy," he assures. "Both now and after."

"Just don't let go of my hand."

In a wry tone, he replies, "If that would please you."

His acceptance grants her the peace and comfort she needs to take the final step forward.

Crossing into the light, it feels like every nerve ending is set on fire. The very atoms of her being tingle as if trying to break themselves free from one another.

Asta follows her, holding her hand as promised, while the light showers them in its radiance.

She smiles as their bodies become nothing more than an outline. They lift into the sky together, just like the other figures they witnessed.

"Until we meet again, my little lamb."

Dragging his palm to her lips, she presses a kiss to the inside. "I look forward to it." Her voice fades as the light grows stronger. Making sure he can hear her, she yells as loud as she can, "And I love you, too, Astamesiophelous!"

They are pulled faster, higher, into the light. Her vision becomes blurry as her skin vibrates.

Marcy's eyes close with laughter, feeling lighter than she ever has before.

In the end, it was all for naught. All the hours, days, and years of her life spent wishing she could die, crying on the bathroom floor, willing herself to cease existing … wasted. But it was gladly wasted.

For once, in the last few moments that count, Marcy wants nothing more than to reexperience human life, unafraid of what comes next. Because no matter what happens, there will always be a piece of Asta within her, loving her, just as much as she loves him.

And for that, she is eternally grateful.

Epilogue

Marianne

Cool air blows from a rattling air conditioning unit, the ribbons attached to the vent waving in the breeze. Mari shudders, rubbing her bare arms in a futile attempt to warm herself up.

How depressing.

She takes in her surroundings, the walls of the brick office building just as frigid as the temperature inside it. She's hard-pressed to complain, however, grateful to have found this job in the first place after her spontaneous move.

Dress shoes thud dully against the carpet, and Mari pinches her shoulder blades back, straightening her posture. She plasters a smile on her face, keeping her hands firmly at her sides.

"Marianne! Lovely to see you again," the man says, extending his hand. "It's a pleasure to welcome you to LevCorp."

Mari takes the man's sweaty hand in her own, shaking it vigorously. "It's a pleasure to be here," she replies, a little too excitedly.

Her awkward tone doesn't deter him. He leads her down endless rows of cubicles, introducing her to people whose names she surely won't remember.

"You will be placed at the end of the hall, where the computers are," he says, gesturing in that direction. His mouth tightens into a bashful smile, his nose becoming dusted in scarlet. "You know, it's a shame to have such a beautiful woman tucked away back there. We seem to separate those with brains and those with beauty in this office. It's a rarity for someone to have both."

With a shy laugh and a wave of her hand, Mari's gaze flicks to the ground. "You flatter me, really. I will be more than happy wherever you put me."

"Oh! I almost forgot!" he exclaims, clapping his hands together. "Before I show you to your desk, I want you to meet my assistant. She will be your point of information for anything related to me. It's imperative you two have a good working relationship."

When they round the corner, Mari is overwhelmed by the massive desk before them. Papers are stacked multiple feet high, with various-colored sticky notes plastered throughout the pages. It all appears extremely disorganized, but she doesn't doubt there is some system in place.

The man takes a step to the side, revealing a woman sitting behind the papers.

"Marianne, I'd like you to meet Ashley," he says while motioning for Mari to approach.

When Ashley stands, Mari tampers down an audible gasp.

Bright blond locks bundled into tight curls sit atop Ashley's head, fastened with a gold pin. Her lips are thin yet pouty, drenched in a saturated apple-red lipstick that complements her deep, caramel brown eyes.

Sticking out her manicured and dainty hand, she says, "I'm Ashley. Nice to meet you, Marianne." Her voice is feminine, even if the words are singsongy.

"Y-you can call me Mari," she sputters, wasting no time embracing this gorgeous woman's soft, inviting hand.

Upon contact, an electric, tingling sensation runs up Mari's spine like lightning. She nearly yelps, and a blush burns hot on her cheeks as she rips her hand away.

What the hell was that?

Gripping the cross necklace at her chest, Mari prays that the tiny piece of metal can cool her smoldering flesh.

But nothing seems to quell the storm brewing inside her. Her heart palpitates, much like it did the day she left her hometown. That nearly made her throw up from nerves, but this is somehow *more* terrifying.

Mari does all she can to hide her thoughts, but she knows they are written clearly across her face.

Ashley beams, tucking a golden curl behind her ear. "Well, then I look forward to working with you, *Mari.*"

Hearing her name on such full, soft lips could make Mari cry. This woman may as well be an angel sent from heaven.

"I'll show you to your cubicle, and you can start your orientation. You'll need to use our office computer for a small portion, so please ask Ashley if you can't find it," the manager says gleefully, guiding Mari away from Ashley's desk.

Thankfully, he didn't seem to notice her eyes bulging out of her head when she ogled his assistant. Or if he did, he doesn't say a word about it.

* * *

The orientation is as bland as Mari expected. They probably thought she is as illiterate with computers as they seem to be, given how new the technology is. Since she finishes quickly, there is plenty of time left in the day for her to be left alone with her thoughts. Thoughts that keep going back to a certain curvaceous, sweet-voiced woman sitting only a stone's throw away.

Mari cradles her face in her hands, feeling the heat radiating against her palms as she's bombarded with impure thoughts.

She never had any luck with dating and rarely feels strongly about the men her mother tries setting her up with. There is always something that makes her turn her nose up at the potential suitors, but her reasonings were shrouded in denial. She knows the reason. She's always known.

The truth shines in her face like a beacon.

I like women.

She can't. She *knows* she can't. Her father is a pastor. Her entire family would shun her — just like they did her uncle — cut out from any gatherings, weddings, or holidays. They view such relationships as vile, unnatural, immoral, and it's even illegal to marry—

A knock comes from behind her.

Nearly falling out of her chair, Mari spins around to face the small opening of her cubicle and greets the one person she hoped it was *not*: Ashley.

Unobstructed by the large desk, Ashley's legs are on full display below the hem of her dress, and Mari looks down, noticing the blood-red stilettos that encase her tiny feet.

God, help me.

Mari swallows hard, but her mouth remains dry. "Ashley, hi," is all she can manage to say.

Ashley appears bothered, but not upset, pressing her lips into a thin line.

"You're new to the city, right?" she asks, her gaze flicking around Mari's barren cube.

Nodding, she answers, "Yeah. I moved into my apartment about a week ago."

Her heels dig into the carpet as Ashley rocks her weight back and forth, nodding profusely. "If you haven't explored the city yet, I'd love to show you around." The tips of her ears go pink, and she quickly adds, "Only if you have no one else, since we'll be working together a lot."

Her laughter, even if nervous, has Mari's heart ricocheting around her rib cage.

Is she asking me out?

If Mari were back home, the chance of this being a date would be a resounding 'no'. But in the city? It's not out of the realm of possibility. Maybe that's why she was drawn here in the first place.

Mari could tell that she was different from everyone in her hometown, but she didn't know exactly why. Meeting Ashley only confirms the longing in her heart, the pull toward something other than the small town and dreary life there. The last shreds of her denial have all but been torn to smithereens.

With so many new emotions brewing, Mari would be a fool to accept Ashley's offer. It would open a can of worms she'd never be able to close, complicating too much of her life. If anything, she should be trying to distance herself from this woman.

But alas, she does not.

With a smile, Mari replies, "I'm free any day except next Friday. I'll be visiting my family for my birthday."

Ashley's lips part in surprise, and her eyes squint with delight. "Is it *on* Friday? Because that's my birthday, too! What a coincidence!" she exclaims with a giggle.

Mari nods, grinning so wide her cheeks hurt. "So, I guess you'll be busy that day, too, huh? How about Saturday?"

A woman as beautiful as Ashley surely has plans, if not a date, but Mari sees no harm in asking. She has no chance to worry, however, as Ashley's response is immediate.

"Free as a bird," she sings, twirling her fingers in time with the notes. Her chest rises and falls, matching the nervousness in her voice.

This is definitely a date.

Mari writes her telephone number on a spare slip of paper, handing it to Ashley as casually as she can in her anxious state.

"Saturday works for me, as well," Mari says, letting out an awkward laugh afterward.

Swiping the paper, Ashley cups it in her palm, clearly pleased with Mari's answer. She steps away, returning to her desk, but quickly turns to look back over her shoulder.

"Do you like apple pie? There's a diner downtown that makes the best in the state," she says, fiddling with the ties of her dress.

Nodding so fast that she sees stars, Mari excitedly exclaims, "I do! It's my favorite dessert!"

Ashley presses her fingers to her lips as her eyes brighten. "Mine too! I'll call you later, 'kay?" she says with joyous laughter before once again leaving for her desk.

As Mari watches Ashley bounce away, her heart swells. She's giddy for the first time in ages, excited at the prospect of going on a proper date.

If Ashley feels the same way … life, family, *everything*, will be complicated.

But then again, Mari has a sneaking suspicion that her greatest love was always meant to be complicated. And that's what makes it worthwhile.

END

About the Author

Nathalia Rui is a hobby writer and artist. She enjoys the monster romance subgenre and is an avid horror fan. In her spare time (when she's not writing), she draws character references and concept art under the careful supervision of her parakeets.

Instagram: @nathalia.rui.author

TikTok: @nathalia.rui.author

For questions, contact: nathalia.rui.author@gmail.com

Also by Nathalia Rui

Captured by the Scaled Outlaw
"Now be a good girl and hold still while I eat you."

After a humiliating demotion, scientist May is sent on a solo mission to the harsh and unforgiving Sandpit Desert – only to be captured by the continent's most wanted eco-terrorist group: Gaia 4.

With her life on the line, May strikes a risky deal with the leader of the group – a towering, hot-headed Lizardfolk named Lowell. Despite his reputation for eating humans, Lowell's interest in May seems to extend beyond the means of simple hunger.

As the two journey together to right a wrong from May's troubled past, danger lurks at every step... but so do the unexpected flames of desire.

Trapped between survival and seduction, May must face a terrifying truth: she and the monster she once feared may not be so different after all.